Win coul
the trees.

Fortunately Kenni wasn't susceptible.

No way!

Animal magnetism aside, Kenni's female intuition was jumping up and down and waving red flags. Sure, he was alluring, and sexy, and too yummy for words, but there was also something fishy about him. He wasn't your run-of-the-mill underachiever, so why was he working in her salon?

And what exactly was Win doing in Magnolia Bluffs? The first thing that came to mind was that he was running from the law. However, since he didn't seem the least bit intimidated by the sheriff, he probably wasn't a fleeing felon. So that left—what?

The whole thing was giving her headaches. And the two ladies who worked for her didn't help matters. Every time Win showed up they turned into giggling loons.

Not that Kenni could blame them. Just the sight of Win Whittaker was enough to make a normal girl drool. And she was one-hundred-percent normal American girl. He almost made her reassess her self-imposed celibacy.

Yikes! What was she thinking?

Dear Reader,

Welcome to my new miniseries featuring Magnolia Bluffs, Georgia—home of peach cobbler, mint juleps and the Permanently Yours Spa. What? You've never heard of Permanently Yours? Why, honey—it's the happenin' place. The perms are curly, the Krispy Kremes are fresh and the rumors are timely. And whether you're in the mood for a blue hair rinse or a cute spiky do, Kenni McAllister's your girl.

Life is good. And then Win Whittaker—tall, dark and sexy—marches into her life and applies for the job of shampoo girl. Puleeze, he's drop-dead gorgeous and charming as all get out, so why is he homeless and unemployed?

In truth, he's a high-powered criminal defense attorney from Washington, D.C., who made a sucker bet with his best friend, and lands in Magnolia Bluffs with barely a penny to his name.

Once Kenni and Win get together, the good times roll. But can a slick urban lawyer really find happiness in a small Southern town? You bet he can, especially when he has his very own sweet Georgia peach.

Writing about small Southern towns is so much fun. I hope you enjoy your trip to Magnolia Bluffs!

Ann

P.S. I love hearing from readers. My mailing address is P.O. Box 97313, Tacoma, WA 98497, and my e-mail address is ann@ann-defee.com. Please write.

GEORGIA
ON HIS MIND
Ann DeFee

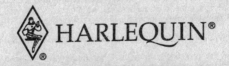

TORONTO • NEW YORK • LONDON
AMSTERDAM • PARIS • SYDNEY • HAMBURG
STOCKHOLM • ATHENS • TOKYO • MILAN • MADRID
PRAGUE • WARSAW • BUDAPEST • AUCKLAND

A big thank-you to some people
who made this book possible:

Barb Gottas, not only are you a good friend,
you're a terrific reader.
Thanks for catching all the stuff I miss.

Amanda Morrow, you work miracles at
keeping my unruly curls under control. Thanks for
sharing your insight into the world of beauty salons.

And Paula Eykelhof, you are the best editor ever!

ISBN-13: 978-0-373-75180-8
ISBN-10:   0-373-75180-X

GEORGIA ON HIS MIND

ABOUT THE AUTHOR

Ann DeFee's debut novel, *A Texas State of Mind* (Harlequin American Romance) was a double finalist in the 2006 Romance Writers of America's prestigious RITA® Awards. Ann writes for both the Harlequin American Romance and Harlequin Everlasting lines. Look for upcoming books.

Drawing on her background as a fifth-generation Texan, Ann loves to take her readers into the sassy and sometimes wacky world of a small Southern community. As an air force wife with twenty-three moves under her belt, she's now settled in her tree house in the Pacific Northwest with her husband, their golden retriever and two very spoiled cats. When she's not writing, you can probably find her on the tennis court or in the park with her walking group.

She'd love to hear from her readers, so please visit her Web site at www.ann-defee.com. Or contact her by snail mail at P.O. Box 97313, Tacoma, WA 98497.

Books by Ann DeFee

HARLEQUIN AMERICAN ROMANCE
1076—A TEXAS STATE OF MIND
1115—TEXAS BORN
1155—SOMEWHERE DOWN IN TEXAS

Don't miss any of our special offers. Write to us at the following address for information on our newest releases.

Harlequin Reader Service
U.S.: 3010 Walden Ave., P.O. Box 1325, Buffalo, NY 14269
Canadian: P.O. Box 609, Fort Erie, Ont. L2A 5X3

HOMEMADE PEACH ICE CREAM

3 cups sugar
4 eggs, beaten
1 quart milk
1 tbsp. vanilla
1 (5-oz) can sweetened condensed milk
2 (12-oz) cans evaporated milk
1 quart sweetened sliced peaches
Sugar to taste
Whole milk
Ice
Rock salt

Combine first 4 ingredients and cook until it thickens. Cool. Add condensed milk and evaporated milk. Blend peaches in blender and add sugar to taste. Add to milk mixture. Pour into 6-quart ice cream freezer and finish filling with whole milk. Fill freezer with ice and rock salt. Churn.

Chapter One

Good grief! Kendrick "Kenni" McAllister resisted the urge to beat her head on the three-way mirror. At five foot nothing and a hundred pounds soaking wet, everything she tried on made her look like she was playing dress-up. Fashion designers obviously didn't cater to folks who were built more like Peter Pan than Paris Hilton.

Kenni glared at the pair of three-inch stilettos in the corner. Combine those instruments of torture with the pink sequined number that would be too long for Naomi Campbell, and well, you could see where this was going.

Jeez, Louise!

Shopping had to be one of the seven circles of hell, but giving up wasn't an option. Kenni had a wedding to attend; and by gosh, she planned to be babe-a-licious if it killed her. However, if today was any indication, her demise might be slow and exceedingly painful.

Using the door as a shield, she peeked out to get her cousin's attention. "Liza, bring me something else. No more sequins, no more bare midriffs and no more ruffles. I need classy and short, very short."

A few seconds later the door popped open and Mary Stuart, cousin number two, flew in with another armload of gowns. Mary's fraternal twin, Liza, was right on her heels. Mary Stuart "Maizie"

Walker and Elizabeth "Liza" Henderson were as physically dis-
similar as the sun and the moon. Liza was petite with dark hair and
big brown eyes. She was gorgeous in an exotic kind of way. Maizie
was tall, blond, voluptuous, and Marilyn-Monroe beautiful.

"Try these on. Swear to goodness, we've looked at every size
two in Atlanta." Maizie waved a hand in the air as she plopped
down on the padded bench. "I think size two should be illegal,
but that's neither here nor there." She tossed Kenni a small
squishy package. "With that black lamé number you'll have to
have these."

"What in tarnation is this?" Kenni ripped open the wrapping
and held up two flesh-colored half-moon bra cups—just the
cups, nothing else.

"They're supposed to be adhesive," Liza offered. "If you hook
them together, they give you cleavage."

Kenni responded with an unladylike snort. "Cleavage? Puh-
leeze, a girl with A-minus bazooms does not now, nor will she
ever, have cleavage."

"Shut up and put 'em on. This—" Liza held up the gown
"—doesn't have a back."

Kenni sighed as she rubbed the bridge of her nose. "You guys
are troupers." They'd accompanied her through every boutique and
department store in Lennox Square, Atlanta's glitziest shopping
center. Plus, they'd endured a sea of sequins, silk, linen, tulle and
something that suspiciously resembled colored cellophane. "No
foolin', I appreciate you giving up a Saturday to do this."

"Are you kidding?" Maizie gave Kenni a playful punch on the
arm. "We have a vested interest in making sure the jerk's tongue
hangs out when he gets a gander at you."

The jerk in question was Walter Harrington, Kenni's ex-
husband. He was also the best man for the upcoming festivities.

"I still have that hideous lavender bridesmaid dress from your
wedding." Liza tossed in that painful reminder.

Kenni didn't mention the fact that her wedding dress resided in a trunk in the attic. Her family assumed that when she and Walter called it quits, she'd ditched everything associated with her ill-fated nuptials.

Wrong. Not that she still hankered for him. On the contrary—her favorite fantasy included a thousand fleas infesting his armpits. She kept the dress merely as a reminder to be very careful in the relationship game. But considering she hadn't had a date in a month of Sundays, her chances of getting involved in a male-female thingy were slim to none.

Talk about depressing.

But back to the mission at hand—finding the perfect dress. The black-sequined number wasn't *even* in the ballpark. Not only was it backless and virtually frontless, it was short enough to be a tennis skirt—minus the bloomers.

"Classy, I want classy with just a hint of sexy." Her proclamation drew dual eye rolls from Maizie and Liza.

Kenni couldn't blame them; she realized she was being difficult. This high-end boutique was not only well out of her price range, it was also her last resort. As the owner and operator of the Permanently Yours Salon in Magnolia Bluffs, Georgia, she wasn't exactly rolling in money.

However, if she could find an outfit that would make Walter rue the day he'd dumped her, she'd be willing to strip down naked and whistle Dixie in the town square. Not that she thought she could make more than a buck fifty doing a striptease—heck, half the girls in the sixth grade had more curves than she did.

"Ladies, I found something in our new inventory." The sales clerk sounded almost as frenzied as Kenni felt.

Not expecting much, Kenni opened the door and encountered Nirvana in the form of a pale pink silk suit—short, short skirt, camisole top and formfitting jacket. The color was ideal for her platinum-blond hair and emerald-green eyes. It was love at first sight.

"Perfect."

KENNI DIDN'T REALIZE the dress was simply the starting point. She had to have shoes, a lacy push-up bra, the perfect earrings and a twenty-dollar pair of hosiery.

"I'd kill for a margarita," Liza uttered as the three ladies left Rich's department store laden with bags.

"Isn't that the truth? Dinner's on me, and we're not going to the food court," Kenni said. "What do you guys think about the Prime Steakhouse?" It was expensive, but it was the least she could do for her two best friends.

"Whoo, hoo!" The twins expressed their approval in unison.

KENNI DEBATED between a strawberry daiquiri and a piña colada but finally decided on the latter. "I want one of those little umbrellas in it," she instructed the waiter.

He was cute, young and best of all, he winked. "Sure. The drinks will be right up."

Kenni flopped back on the leather seat. She was exhausted, her feet hurt and her spiky hairdo had long since passed trendy and was rapidly heading toward dumpy. Not to mention she was working on a raging headache. Fortunately, or unfortunately, her cousins didn't look much better.

"Did our boutique experience remind you of the dress-up box Aunt Eugenie gave us for Christmas when we were what, nine or ten?" Elizabeth asked her sister.

"I think we were ten," Maizie answered.

Kenni knew exactly how old she was when she first spied the dress-up box. It was indelibly imprinted in her brain because it was the first Christmas after Mama died, and she moved in with Eugenie and Annie Belle Carpenter.

"I'll never forget the look on your face when Mom gave you the dress-up box." Maizie and Liza's mother, Eleanor, was the third Carpenter sister. "Gosh, we were teenagers by that time and you were just a little squirt." The twins were six years older than Kenni and they had always treated her like a favorite little sister. Although they weren't Kenni's cousins by blood, Maizie and Liza were relatives of the soul.

Just the thought of the dress-up box sent Kenni's memories spiraling back to the night her mama didn't return to the single-wide they called home. Kenni finally cried herself to sleep, and the next day Mama still wasn't home. So like a good little girl, she ate her Cocoa Puffs and trudged to the school bus stop. Once or twice the thought flitted through her mind that Mama might not ever come home again. That couldn't happen! Mama was her only family.

Then during recess she broke down and confided in her teacher, Mrs. Christiansen. Just the thought of going back to that dark empty trailer scared her witless.

Before Kenni knew it, the school principal, Mr. Bayliss, was holding her hand and they were standing on the porch of the prettiest house in town. When she and Mama used to walk to the grocery store they always stopped at the white picket fence and admired the place. Mama would say, "One day, honey, we'll live in a house like that."

Kenni never really believed her, but there she was on a front porch that was bigger than their whole trailer. And the front door—Lordy mercy—it was gigantic!

Then it hit her like a ton of bricks. This was an orphanage! *No, no, no way!* But where else did little kids go when their mamas went missing? Kenni had a death grip on her school bag. Young as she was, she'd already read Dickens, and by gosh, an orphanage wasn't a place she wanted to visit, let alone live.

Don't, don't wet yourself. Kenni was concentrating so hard she didn't quite understand what Mr. Bayliss was saying. She did hear the chime as it echoed through the house.

Kenni jumped backward when the door creaked open, revealing a woman who was almost as round as she was tall. She had the prettiest smile on her chubby face.

"Land's sakes child, come in, come in. I'm Cora," she said as she called back over her shoulder. "Miss Anna Belle, Miss Eugenie, our little guest is here."

"Mosey on back to the kitchen now, ya hear. I have a fresh pot of coffee brewing for you, Mr. Bayliss. And I have some chocolate chip cookies right out of the oven." She winked at Kenni. "I bet you like cookies, don't you?"

Kenni managed a nod. At this point even a small smile was impossible, so she was grateful the woman kept up the chatter. That way she didn't have to talk.

Cora led the way down the wide center hall of the antebellum home to a kitchen at the back of the house. And what a kitchen! Kenni almost swallowed her tongue. She'd seen places like this in magazines—gleaming copper pans hanging over an island at least the size of Hawaii, an acre of spotless red brick floor, and the appliances—holy moley—they could feed an army out of this place.

"Sit down and I'll get those cookies. My, oh, my, you're going to love my goodies." Cora toddled over to the stove and expertly flipped the chocolate morsels from the cookie sheet to a cooling rack. "Miss Anna Belle and Miss Eugenie will be down in two shakes of a lamb's tail. They've been fussin' over that room for hours."

Almost simultaneous to her proclamation, a wiggly mass of white fur with a black button nose jumped into Kenni's lap and bathed her face in puppy kisses.

She couldn't help herself; a giggle bubbled up. No matter how bad things got, she couldn't resist a puppy.

"Looks like you've met Ruffles." Kenni recognized that slow

Southern drawl—it was Miss Carpenter, one of the fifth-grade teachers. She was tiny and blond, like Mama, but older.

"I don't know if you remember me, I'm Anna Belle Carpenter," she said, squatting down to stroke Ruffles' fur. "My sister Eugenie will be here in a minute."

"Miss Anna Belle, can I fix you up a nice glass of iced tea?" Cora asked, bustling around the kitchen.

"I'll get it myself. Why don't you sit down with us?" Anna Belle asked Cora while gently pushing a lock of hair off Kenni's face. "Cora takes good care of us. If you ever need anything, you can always ask her. And as you can tell, she makes a mean cookie."

What was the lady talking about? It was all so confusing! Kenni's trailer was clear across town, why would she make that kind of trip to get a cookie? And more importantly, where was Mama?

"I can't stay. Mama will be worried when she gets home and I'm not there." Kenni could tell from the looks on the grown-ups' faces they didn't agree. "Really, I can walk. You don't even have to drive me."

"Don't you worry, not one little bit. We'll tell your mama where you are." The voice belonged to a tall man with a kind smile and a huge gun planted on his hip. His companion was also tall and she was one of the most beautiful creatures Kenni had ever seen.

The dark-haired woman leaned over to speak to Kenni. "You're going to stay with us for a while. I'm Miss Eugenie and this is Sheriff Madison. Would you like to sit in my lap while I tell you something?" she asked.

"No, ma'am. I'm just fine where I am." Something terrible had happened. Kenni knew that as well as she knew her own name. Would it go away if she ignored it? Probably not.

Then when Miss Eugenie and the sheriff gave each other another one of those grown-up looks, Kenni knew deep down in her soul her life was about to change. That's when one fat tear rolled down her cheek.

"Kenni, sweetie," Miss Eugenie said, taking her hand. "Your mom was hit by a car when she was walking home last night. She's in the hospital. We didn't know you were by yourself until this morning. I think everyone assumed you were at a babysitter's." She patted Kenni's hand. "A nice policeman went by your house and knocked, but no one answered. Were you afraid to go to the door?"

Kenni nodded. She really wished she could stop crying, but she couldn't.

"I'm sorry you had to stay by yourself, but you won't be alone again. I promise. You're going to live with us. Is that okay with you?"

All Kenni could do was nod. She didn't want to spend the night at the trailer alone. "Can I see her?" She couldn't help ending her question with a sniff.

"Just as soon as she feels better we'll take you to the hospital," the sheriff assured her.

Although the words should have been comforting, the expression on his face was grim. But maybe that was the way he always looked.

"For now, we'd like you to stay with Miss Anna Belle and Miss Eugenie."

"I don't know. Mama doesn't know these people."

The sheriff gave Mr. Bayliss another one of those looks.

"Kenni, sweetie…"

Uh-oh, big trouble. A principal never called a kid "sweetie."

"Your mother knows and trusts me, and I certainly wouldn't ask you to do something she wouldn't like. You realize that, don't you?"

"Yes, I guess," Kenni admitted reluctantly.

"Great. Now that's settled."

Miss Eugenie smiled as she took Kenni's hand. "Why don't you bring Ruffles with you and we'll show you your room. We're so glad you're staying with us."

Miss Anna Belle and Miss Eugenie kept talking as they led the way upstairs to a bedroom so grand Kenni was sure she'd stepped into a fairy tale. It was a little girl's dream come true with a four-poster bed, yellow flowered wallpaper and a sea of white eyelet.

Kenni had to force her mouth shut. She was so confused. This room obviously belonged to a princess, and princesses didn't live in a mobile home park.

THAT WAS THE BEGINNING of the next chapter in Kenni's life. Several days later, the sheriff, Miss Eugenie and Miss Anna Belle took her to the hospital. As Kenni stood in her mother's room watching the equipment beep and buzz, her heart sank to the tips of her toes. Mama wasn't ever coming home.

"Sweetie, come here," Mama whispered.

Kenni leaned close so she could hear. "What, Mama?"

"You know I love you more than anything, don't you?" She squeezed Kenni's hand.

"I know." Tears rolled down Kenni's cheeks.

"I want the best for you."

"Uh-huh."

"I talked to these nice ladies, and I want you to live with them. Everything will be fine, I promise."

"Yes, Mama." Kenni wanted to throw her arms around her mother's neck, but there were too many machines and tubes in the way.

"Please be happy. You're my little love."

"I love you, too."

"I know." Her mother's response was barely a whisper. "Be a good girl. Now go with Miss Carpenter and remember I love you."

"I'll remember," Kenni whispered as she followed Anna Belle out of the room.

"Mama's dying, isn't she?" It was a question Kenni had to

ask even though she knew her heart would break when she heard the answer.

Miss Anna Belle made soothing little circles on her palm. "Yes, sweetheart, I'm afraid she is. But she knows we'll take good care of you. Remember how she said she loves you, and she wants you to live with us and have a happy life?"

"Yes." Kenni somehow managed to answer through her tears.

"That's because she knows we'll do everything we can to make you happy. Right, sister?"

Miss Eugenie nodded and gave Kenni one of her slow, beautiful smiles.

"We'll never try to replace your mother, but we are so happy you'll be living with us," Miss Anna Belle said.

WITH THE INNOCENCE and wisdom of childhood, Kenni realized that everything would be okay. Much later she learned that Anna Belle and Eugenie had petitioned for guardianship, and it had been expedited through the court system. Things like that happened in small towns. It was especially fortunate that Anna Belle and Eugenie's cousin was the superior court judge.

After Eugenie married Sheriff Dave Madison and moved into the house next door, Anna Belle took over as Kenni's primary guardian. Later Anna Belle also married and the sisters decided it was time to make the adoption permanent. Since Anna Belle and her husband, Joe Nunn, were living in the Carpenter family home, they decided to become Kenni's official parents.

So as much as Kenni loved and missed her mother, she experienced a wonderful childhood in the arms of her adoptive family. She had two beloved sets of parents.

How lucky could a girl get?

Chapter Two

"Are you drowning your sorrows, or are you just really thirsty?" The speaker laughed as he slapped Winston Andrew Whittaker IV on the back.

Win glanced at the row of empty beer bottles. His law partner, Colby Wharton, was one of the biggest smart alecks in D.C., but this time he'd hit the nail on the head. Win *had* been drowning his sorrows. It was a good thing his house was only a few blocks away; at least he could stumble home without being arrested.

"I don't consider it any of your business, but I was trying to formulate a plan for world peace," Win proclaimed as he took another long swallow. His favorite pub, the Hair of the Hound, was the watering hole for a good number of the Yuppies who lived in the upscale D.C. neighborhood of Georgetown. The owner had transported an entire English pub lock, stock and tap from a village in the Cotswolds. It featured dark paneling, battle-scarred tables, the vague scent of wood smoke and eight hundred different brands of beer. Although Win didn't intend to sample all eight hundred, he did plan to wade through quite a few of the brews.

"I'm getting a mixed message here." Colby waved his hand indicating the empty bottles. "You won the case this afternoon. However, from the looks of this mess you'd think you lost."

"I should have. The senator's punk kid was guilty as sin.

When the jury announced the verdict, he had the gall to giggle and wink at me. He winked at me!"

"We're criminal defense attorneys. Sometimes we're responsible for getting guilty people off. It's the nature of the game. Don't you remember what they said in law school? Everyone has the right to a good defense."

Colby didn't bother to elaborate on the fact that Wharton and Whittaker was the best and most expensive law firm in the District of Columbia metropolitan area, including the surrounding areas of Virginia and Maryland.

Win absently arranged the empty bottles by height. "Did you know the man he ran into had a house full of kids?"

The teenager had admitted he'd been drinking and speeding when he T-boned a cab, killing the driver. Although Win got the boy off on a technicality, he'd bet his Porsche that within a week the spoiled brat would be sloshed and behind the wheel again. And why not? If the kid got into trouble, Daddy would get him off, just like he'd done this time.

"I hated that case," Win proclaimed, as he grabbed a handful of peanuts. He had to get something in his stomach besides alcohol or he'd regret it in the morning.

Colby put his chin on his fist and stared at his partner. "You know what your problem is?"

"Nope, but I'm sure you're about to tell me." Win's snide comment was lost on the guy.

"Bet your sweet butt, I am. You're suffering from burnout. Up to now, you've always had it too easy. You went to the best schools in the country and you have a trust fund that equals the GNP of several third-world nations. You have good looks, brains and a bloodline that goes back to the *Mayflower*. You have it made, but you feel there's something missing. Something you need to experience."

"Your point being?"

Colby gave him the stare that had always been a prelude to trouble. "My point is that you need to get in touch with your inner 'Joe Six-Pack'."

"Like your family's poor," Win said with a snort.

"You're right. But I grew up in a small town so I knew people from a variety of backgrounds. My best friend's old man was in jail for armed robbery and his mother worked in a convenience store. For them, keeping the electricity on was a challenge."

Colby paused as if pondering the situation. "In fact, watching them scrimp and save to pay an attorney was one of the reasons I was so adamant about establishing our pro bono program. And with that in mind, I have a bet," he said with a mischievous grin.

Uh-oh! They'd started making wagers when they were roommates in law school and invariably Win ended up on the losing side.

"What?" Even giving voice to the question was dangerous.

"You remember all those stories I told you about Magnolia Bluffs?"

How could Win forget? Every time Colby had more than a couple of beers in his belly, he prattled on about his hometown, Magnolia Bluffs, Georgia. It was the last place on the planet Win wanted to visit.

"Yeah?" he answered.

Colby leaned back, a smirk dancing across his face.

A smirk! This had all the earmarks of something seriously bad.

"Here are the stakes. If I win, you coerce some of our bar association colleagues to do more pro bono work, *and* you fix me up with your sister. Every time I ask her out, she comes up with a lame excuse. How many times can a woman paint her nails?"

It was Win's turn to smirk. "Wonder what Kristen's thinking? Could it be that she remembers the one and only date you guys had? The time you tied one on and ended up puking on the sidewalk…? Hmm. Do you suppose that turned her off?"

"I was nervous. Come on, use your charm to convince her I'm a reformed man. I know you can do it."

"I don't know." Win shook his head, simply to tease his friend. Colby was one of the nicest guys in town.

"If you win, we'll change the name of the firm to Whittaker and Wharton. We'll do the letterhead, the business cards, the whole deal."

Convincing their colleagues to do anything that would impact their bottom line would be challenging, and Kristen would rather date Godzilla than go out with Colby, but the idea of changing the name of the firm *was* appealing. The only reason it was currently named Wharton and Whittaker was the result of a bad coin toss, so a bet was sort of karmic.

"Okay, what are you proposing?"

"I want you to start over, at least for a little while. See if you can make it without anything but a few bucks in your pocket. That way you can experience how some of our more unfortunate clients live." The more he talked, the more Colby got into the spirit of the game.

"Here's the deal. You show up in Magnolia Bluffs with only two hundred dollars to your name. It has to last you a full month or until you get a job. No credit cards, no car, and no fair using your education or connections. There'll be just two hundred dollars standing between you and starvation."

Of all the wacky ideas Colby had ever come up with—and they were legion—this was the topper, but Win decided to play along.

"Okay, I have a couple of questions. First, what about your parents? What are they going to think if they see me walking the streets of Magnolia Bluffs?"

"No problem. They're on an around-the-world cruise. They won't be back for a couple of months."

One excuse down—one to go. "What about our workload? Can you guys handle everything without me?"

Colby gave him one of those "are you kidding" looks. "We've tied up most of our big cases, and besides that, you haven't had a vacation in years," he said. "I think it's more important for you to regain some enthusiasm for our profession than for us to take on a new case. So yes, we'll do fine without you for a month or so."

There was something to be said for renewing his professional passion. "Does that hometown of yours have a McDonald's?" If all else failed, surely he could get a job at Mickey D's.

"Nope," Colby said, grinning ear to ear. "And here's the rest of the deal. At the end of June there's a big garden party put on by the Historical Society. If you can get invited to that—and going as a waiter doesn't count—you win. If you don't, I'm the victor."

How hard could it be to get invited to a party? Win was on the D.C. society A-list. But they were discussing *Magnolia Bluffs, Georgia,* and he had a suspicion he had just signed on to the biggest sucker bet of all time. Colby had had the hots for Kristen a very long time.

"I'll give you fair warning, a garden party invitation is something folks work years to get. They don't let just *anyone* in. Even as handsome as you are, you'll have a hard time crackin' that nut."

Damn him! Colby knew there wasn't anything like a dare to get Win's juices flowing.

He tipped his bottle in a salute to friendship and a good bet. "You're on, buddy. Here's to the garden party."

Chapter Three

Yep, Win had been snookered. What in the hell had he been thinking? He had a law practice, a home and a life. So what was he doing on a Greyhound bus sharing a seat with a guy who had only a marginal acquaintance with personal hygiene?

The whole thing had been pretty much of a lark until he'd landed in Atlanta—that was when he'd put two and two together and got a whoppin' big six. The inventory of his personal possessions included a driver's license (no way could he buy a car—shoot, he couldn't afford a spark plug), the aforementioned two hundred dollars (and forty-seven cents), and a duffel bag containing a couple of pairs of well-worn jeans and some old T-shirts. With that wardrobe, he'd be lucky to get a job washing dishes.

"This is it," his seat companion said. The man had come out of his stupor and was pointing at something out the window.

"What?" Win asked.

"That's Magnolia Bluffs, the place you said you were going."

"Oh yeah, thanks." Win picked up his bag from the grimy floor as the bus belched to a stop in front of a run-down hotel. The peeling paint and listing veranda notwithstanding, Win could see that at one time, the Magnolia Inn had been a bastion of gentility and big-hat tea parties. It must have fallen on hard times because now it doubled as the bus station and the Western Union office.

He grimaced as he stepped off the vehicle into a wall of heat and humidity. Good God, it was hot, and it was only late spring. D.C. was bad, but this was stifling. Win wiped the sweat off his forehead.

Gut up, you can do this. And that quickly became his mantra.

The inside of the terminal was only slightly better than the outside. The ancient air conditioner wasn't keeping up with the heat. Win strolled over to the snack bar and sat down on one of the cracked vinyl seats at the counter.

"What can I do for ya?" The waitress was friendly, but definitely had that "rode hard and put away wet" look. Good God, where had that come from?

"A big iced tea, please."

"Sure enough, hon." She was back in a few moments with a glass that contained at least a gallon of amber liquid.

"Anything to eat?" she asked.

Actually, he'd love a cheeseburger, but his priorities were, a job first and superfluous things like food second.

"Nope. Not right now. Thank you."

"Sure, hon. I can't blame you there." The waitress hitched a hip and leaned on the counter. "Lord in heaven, it's too hot to eat. We don't normally sweat up like this until August."

"Really?"

"You ain't from around here, are you, sugar?"

"Nope. Virginia." He presumed that was close enough to the Mason-Dixon Line to be acceptable.

"Always wanted to go up that direction, but I've never been north of Gatlinburg. I went up there once with my first husband." She tapped her front tooth. "Or was that my second?"

Did she really expect an answer?

"Oh well, never mind. Let me know if you need anythin' else, ya hear?" She started to wipe the counter.

"Well, Mabel, there is one thing." Win had noticed the name

tag pinned to the front of her pink uniform. "Do you know anyone who needs an employee?"

"Depends. What do you know how to do?"

That was a good question. While Win was intimately familiar with writs of habeas corpus, restraining orders and arraignment procedures, he couldn't list many practical skills.

"I don't know."

Obviously it wasn't the answer Mabel was expecting. She scratched her head before speaking. "Seems like I heard Harley down at the service station is looking for someone to change oil. Any guy worth his salt can do that."

Talk about a good way to impugn his manhood. He normally took his Porsche to the dealer for routine maintenance so obviously auto mechanics wasn't one of his long suits. But how hard could it be?

"Where can I find Harley?"

Mabel pointed out the front door. "Take a right and go up past the courthouse square, then turn left at the Confederate soldier. That's Main Street. Harley's place is two blocks up on the right. You can't miss it. It's the Texaco station."

He probably could—miss it, that is. Especially since he'd die of heat prostration before he got there.

"Thanks." Win finished off the tea and left a hefty tip. That habit would have to come to a screeching halt. "I'll tell him Mabel sent me."

"Sure enough, hon, you do that."

No wonder people in the South walked so slowly; he'd only ambled half a block, yet he felt like he'd been wrapped in Saran Wrap and put in a slow-bake oven. He was tempted to stick himself with a fork to see if he was done.

But when in Rome, etc., so he strolled down the tree-lined street appreciating the quaintness of his home for the next month.

That is if he could find someplace to stay, a way to earn money, and something decent to eat.

That proved to be easier said than done.

THE STITCHED NAME on the shirt said Harley. The owner of the garment was beefy, bald and short-tempered. "If you don't know how to change oil, I can't use you." He made the statement right before he rolled back under an Olds Cutlass that had seen better days.

Scratch that one. Three hours later, Win had also been turned down for a job at the Temptee Freeze (their workforce was limited to young, nubile blondes), Dale's Supermarket (Ed's cousin had been hired to do the stocking), and as a dishwasher at the Urban Diner. That one really frosted him. First of all, there was nothing even remotely urban about the place; and second, the middle-aged female owner made some crude remark about his rear end and then said that he was too "purty." Claimed he'd be a distraction to the waitresses.

The folks in Magnolia Bluffs were obviously *not* familiar with sexual discrimination laws.

It was almost five o'clock, and things were looking grim. No job, no lodging, and very little money—crap! The only bright spot in his day was that he was about to solve his hunger problem with a bag of day-old fried chicken and a thirty-two-ounce Big Gulp. He hoped to God it didn't kill him. The good thing was that the entire meal had only set him back a dollar seventy-five.

Win had noticed a gazebo in the center of the park. There were benches, it was private and it seemed perfect for an impromptu picnic. And if he was really lucky, the cops wouldn't bust him for loitering. At least if he went to jail he'd get three hots and a cot—and wasn't that a pitiful thought.

Even though the chicken was greasy and cold, he cleaned the bones like a buzzard dining on roadkill. When dusk brought a welcome cool breeze, Win kicked back and savored the sweet smell of newly cut grass and the sound of kids playing in the park. It had been a long time since he'd felt so relaxed.

Perchance there was something to be said for the slow and easy Southern rhythm….

Who did he think he was kidding? He was a city boy, through and through.

Win briefly considered calling off the bet. Nope, he wasn't a quitter. And he'd rather face a nest of pit vipers than arrange a date between Kristen and Colby. Those two idiots were like oil and water.

So discounting the idea of losing the wager, Win checked his limited assets. The meager number of bills in his hand-tooled Italian wallet was enough to make a grown man cry. Simply put—he needed a game plan ASAP, and the first item on that list was a fleabag hotel, preferably minus the bedbugs. He tossed the empty packet into the garbage and retraced his steps to the Magnolia Inn.

MORNING FOUND HIM back at his favorite park bench munching on a half-dead banana and slugging back a quart of milk. He felt horrible. No wonder—he hadn't had *any* sleep. The mattress was as hard as a Mayan sacrificial altar, and the constant rhythmic banging on the wall next to his headboard was enough to induce permanent insomnia.

Win was trying to figure out his options when he saw potential salvation. The hand-lettered sign, Shampoo Girl Wanted, Apply Within, was in the window of an establishment that screamed girly-girl. Everything from the pink-and-white striped awning, to the flower boxes with trailing coral geraniums, to the Permanently Yours written in gold script was Southern belle at its finest.

Shampooing a bunch of strangers sounded about as appealing as cleaning portable loos, but Win was desperate. He washed his own hair every morning. How hard could the job be?

Win chugged the rest of the milk and marched across the street. In a thousand years of bad fantasies he'd never considered stooping to anything this ignominious; but hey, it was better than sloppin' hogs. Wearing his best courtroom smile, Win strolled into Permanently Yours. He'd charmed hundreds of juries, so how difficult could it be to convince the owner of a salon in Podunk, Georgia, to hire him?

Regrettably, the answer to that question, ladies and gentlemen of the jury, would probably be—pretty damn hard.

Chapter Four

"Okay, folks, we have a busy day and we're still shorthanded, so—" Kenni paused "—if you'll just hang in with me I promise we'll get some help soon." Their daily staff meeting usually degenerated into a gossip fest. What did she expect when the "staff" consisted of her two wackiest friends?

Raylene Yarborough was the darling of the blue-haired set—that girl could process the tightest perm in all Georgia. And then there was Tallulah Tucker—just call her Toolie—an expatriate from a posh Atlanta salon and a favorite of the avant-garde girls.

"Hon," Raylene said, popping her gum in rhythm to a Martina McBride tune, "have you managed to round up a date for the wedding?"

Kenni sighed. Business always played second fiddle to chitchat and today wasn't any different.

"No, and how much shampoo do we need to order?"

"Really? Time's a-wastin'." Raylene fluffed her already big hair. "Toolie, hon, you know any eligible men?"

"How about conditioner?" Kenni asked, even though she knew that trying to change the subject would be like trying to turn back the tide.

"Are you kidding? All the guys of my acquaintance, sort of,

you know, like bat for the other team." Toolie raised her eyebrows for emphasis.

"What does our client list look like for today?"

Raylene and Toolie were so busy trying to micromanage her social life they didn't bother to answer.

"And everyone I know is either a redneck or married. I don't know which is worse," Raylene said with a pout.

"That's it! Read my lips. I *do not* need a date for the wedding. I don't mind going by myself."

Raylene and Toolie stared, astounded at her audacious declaration.

"And don't look at me like that!" Aargh! The ditzy duo meant well, but when they started meddling they made her crazy.

"Holy cow, would you take a gander at that." Raylene had wandered over to the front window and was watching something, or someone, in the park across the street.

Toolie joined her friend. "Now that's what I call eye candy."

"Kenni, come here, girl. You've got to see this." When Raylene put her mind to something she was like a pit bull gnawing on a bone.

"No! We have business to discuss."

Raylene and Toolie were practically plastered to the window. "Well lookie, lookie. Oh, my goodness, I'm about to swoon." When Raylene fanned her face, Kenni realized she was fighting a losing battle.

"Are you sure you don't want a lookie-loo," Toolie taunted. "Great black hair and that bad-boy look you dig—T-shirt, tight jeans and scuffed boots. Yummy, yummy." She emphasized the point by licking her lips.

"Hush up. You two sound like you're in middle school."

"Ooh, dude. He just stood up and is he ever built," Toolie continued her running commentary.

"I'm havin' a flash of light." Raylene tapped a crimson nail on her forehead.

"What you're havin' is a stroke. Now, both of you get over here so we can finish our business. We have to get this shop open."

"I'm gonna run and see if we can hire him to take you to the wedding."

"Over my dead body!" Kenni was about to panic. They really were capable of pulling that kind of harebrained stunt.

"Great idea," Toolie agreed. "Make sure he has all his teeth. We can find him something to wear and make him presentable. With that bone structure and the right clothes, he'll look like a million bucks."

"No!" Kenni screeched. "I don't need a date, and if I did…" Her rant was interrupted in midstream by Raylene's next comment.

"Well, ladies, it looks like we're about to see him up close and personal. He's headin' this way."

"Good grief!" Kenni watched in fascination. It felt like everything was moving in slow motion.

The bell above the door tinkled its happy little greeting. Funny, Kenni thought, that used to seem cheerful, but now it sounded more like a psychotic elf banging on a tin can.

"Ladies," he said, with the slightest hint of a Southern accent. She got the impression that if he'd been wearing a cap, he would have tipped it.

"I think you might have a job for me."

Oh, boy. If he could bottle that grin he'd make a million bucks. Then his comment hit Kenni right between the eyes. And if Raylene's bugged-out eyes were any indication, she'd received the same message. Toolie merely giggled.

"Uh, well, um, it's like this." Kenni had no clue what it was like. Although she'd graduated cum laude with a degree in English, she was being amazingly monosyllabic.

"Well, sugar, I don't think…"

The tall, dark and devastatingly handsome stranger interrupted Raylene. "I know I can do the job." He winked. "It can't be that hard, and I'm sure the ladies will love me."

On that note, Kenni almost swallowed her tongue. No way would she hop off to the wedding with a hired date—no matter how good-looking. "I'm sorry, I don't think so."

The man looked genuinely puzzled. "Is it because I'm a guy?"

"Huh?"

"Well, I mean, how hard can it be to give someone a shampoo? I'm a hard worker and I don't have very many vices. How about this? I work free for a couple of days. That way you can try me out without it costing you a cent."

Glory be! The guy was applying for the shampoo girl job. Talk about feeling like an idiot. Even more disturbing was the fact that Kenni found herself agreeing to his plan.

"You're on. Work today for free and then we can talk." Where had that come from? "Raylene, why don't you get all his particulars like name, address, social security number, etc?"

"Thanks, that's great," he said, with the now-familiar grin.

Kenni hesitated before she took the hand he offered. Her stomach did a backflip when she touched him. Somehow, some way she felt sure this decision was going to change her life.

She hoped to goodness it wouldn't be a huge mistake.

Chapter Five

Even though the day had started out on a sucky note—her alarm didn't go off, the garbage disposal backed up, and her cat left a dead mouse on the back porch—and despite the fact that every woman who walked in the salon was drooling over the new employee, Kenni was determined to maintain her dignity and decorum. That was until Raylene dropped the bomb—their shampoo guy was homeless. What next, an infestation of cicadas?

"Homeless? What makes you think that?"

"How about the fact he's using the Magnolia Inn as an address?"

"Oh, my word!" Kenni exclaimed. "What if he's wanted by the law? We could be arrested as accomplices, or accessories after the fact, or whatever."

"You're a weird woman," Raylene informed her. "There's nothing wrong with that man except he's down on his luck. My intuition tells me he's perfectly fine, and as you know," she preened, "my female antenna is never wrong."

"That's why you've been married three times?"

Raylene stuck out her tongue. "Don't get smart with me, girl. Just look at that." She was referring to the gorgeous man who was chatting up Viola Horatio while he washed her shoe-polish-black hair.

"Merciful heavens, how much shampoo is he using? He has enough bubbles to do a rerun of Lawrence Welk," Kenni exclaimed.

"Not to worry. If he makes Morticia happy that makes me downright giddy. She's actually smiling and that old bat hasn't cracked a grin in the last decade."

Kenni suppressed a giggle. When Raylene was right, she was right. Viola Horatio had the tightest "cheeks" in all Georgia.

For years they had been trying to convince her to go for a color that was a bit closer to nature—but so far, no luck. She liked her Morticia look, complete with a streak of snow-white hair.

Viola and her husband Percy were the Mutt and Jeff of Magnolia Bluffs and they were frequently the hottest topic of gossip. Their latest escapade involved her chasing him around the city park with a skillet. Rumor had it she'd found him kissing the choir director in the basement of the Methodist church. That was when she decided to play some "Amazing Grace" on his noggin.

Poor Mr. Horatio.

"HOW ARE YOU DOING, Miz Thornton?" Kenni asked, greeting her next client. She was about to snap the black plastic cape around the woman's wrinkled neck, but stopped when she heard a noise up front.

"I'll be right back," she said, patting Mrs. Thornton's thin shoulder. Some of the seniors tended to get upset when anything deviated from the norm, and whatever was happening in the reception area sounded like it was way outside the ordinary.

"Hey, yo, open that cash drawer!" The man's slurred demand was almost obliterated by the sound of Toolie squealing.

Damn, that girl was loud!

WIN WAS TRYING to determine the difference between a lanolin hair mask and a deep conditioner when he heard a scream. Mrs. Horatio jumped straight out of the chair.

Something was wrong. If this had been D.C., he would have automatically assumed it was a drive-by shooting.

"Stay where you are," Win instructed, sprinting toward the front of the salon. What he saw when he rounded the corner was not good, not good at all. This was Mayberry, U.S.A.; so what was a dude doing with a tea towel over his face and waving a gun?

Robbing the joint, that's what. Crap!

When Toolie screamed, Win slid to an immediate halt. He couldn't go unprepared into the middle of a potential bloodbath. He had to have a plan.

Think. Think. Think.

Weapons? Nope. The most lethal thing he had in his arsenal was a can of hairspray.

Brains? Yep. He had plenty, and considering the situation, he needed every particle of gray matter he could muster.

"Here, here take it all." The voice belonged to his cute little blond boss. How had she made it to the front so fast?

Toolie finally stopped screeching. Thank you, God!

Win took another peek and noticed that even though Kenni was shoving a handful of bills at the robber, he was still screaming obscenities. The guy was a meth head, no doubt about it. At best, they were treacherously erratic; at their worst, they were homicidal. This was a dangerous situation.

"Um, what are we going to do?" Raylene whispered.

Win had been so focused on the crime that he almost jumped out of his skin when she tapped him on the shoulder. As his heart resumed its normal cadence he had a stroke of genius. Some wise man had said that necessity was the mother of invention, and this situation definitely fell into the category of a "mother."

Win put a finger to his lips in the universal sign for silence and waved the ladies, who were creeping forward, back to the rear of the salon.

"Call 911," he whispered to a woman who had enough foil in

her hair to pick up radio waves. She nodded as she scooted toward Kenni's office.

Win grabbed the fire extinguisher and was heading toward the front of the shop when he realized he wasn't alone. He glanced over his shoulder and found Raylene right behind him.

"I'm going with you," she mouthed.

"No," he mouthed back.

"Think again, buster."

And that's how Win ended up with a sidekick who looked more like Dolly Parton than Barney Fife.

Damn—at least Barney had *one* bullet.

"You make a commotion to get his attention while I crawl behind the counter. Then I'll spray him with this." He indicated the extinguisher. "You okay with that?"

Raylene nodded.

The situation was rapidly escalating out of control. No matter what Kenni said or did, the man became more agitated. Please, God, he wouldn't start shooting. Waiting for the cops was no longer an option.

Raylene tapped Win and whispered, "Now?"

"Now," he replied as he got down on his hands and knees to make the crawl across the floor. It was no more than ten feet, but it looked as broad as the Sahara.

Although Win didn't regularly darken the doors of his neighborhood church, this situation called for some praying. Heavenly intervention was a good thing—especially when he was dealing with a potential hostage situation, and that's exactly what was going to happen if a deputy dog stumbled in the door.

Win gave his accomplice the high sign and readied himself.

KENNI WAS ATTEMPTING to calm things when chaos broke out. At least that's what it sounded like. Actually, it was Raylene beating on something and screaming like a banshee. What *did* she think she was doing? Agitating this guy was not going to help, not when he was waving a gun.

Then Kenni spied her newest employee crawling toward a glass counter containing hair products. Okay, she got it—frontal distraction, rear attack.

"What the hell, man?" the meth head muttered as he redirected his gun toward the back of the shop.

It was now or never, Kenni thought as she grabbed the pepper spray from under the counter. Toolie had a deer-in-the-headlights look as she watched Kenni shake the can.

"Hey, stupid, this way," Kenni yelled. When the bad guy spun around, she let him have it right in the face. He let out a horrendous scream, prompting Win to jump from behind the counter and finish him off with a dousing of chemical foam.

It was teamwork at its finest. The icing on the cake was when Raylene and Toolie decided to give the old boy a big-time whoopin'.

"I got the gun," Win said, holding up the weapon. "I think he messed with the wrong folks."

"No kiddin'," Raylene agreed, as she plopped her ample rear on the intruder's body and then bounced a couple of times for good measure. "We've got woman power." She polished her nails on her chest and grinned.

"Ever thang okay in here?" Patrolman Booty Carter asked as he strolled in the front door. In a previous life Booty had been one of the best tackles in Magnolia Bluffs High football history. In this incarnation, his girth leaned more toward paunch than punch.

"We're okay. He's not doing as well," Kenni said, indicating the man on the floor.

"Hey, Miss Raylene. Whatcha got down there?"

The perp groaned when she bounced again. "This guy tried to rob us, rob us! I want you to throw the book at him, ya' hear me."

"Yes, ma'am, we'll see what we can do," Booty replied, snapping the cuffs on the perp.

"Take me in. Now, man." The whiny request came from Raylene's captive.

Booty was wearing a great big grin until Win spoke.

"Officer, I have the gun." He held the firearm out with two fingers.

Police procedure in Magnolia Bluffs was as different from D.C. as night and day. Back home if the cops encountered a guy with a gun he would have been spread-eagled on the ground before he could blink. In the Magnolia Bluffs scenario, the policeman simply took the weapon.

As nice as the good-old-boy network might seem, police work down South was a bit too casual for Win's taste. That type of negligence got people killed.

Chapter Six

"Oh. My. Gawd," Toolie squealed. "That was so…that was so…"
She couldn't seem to finish her thought before she fell into the
nearest chair.

"Is it okay for us to come out now?" The disembodied voice
belonged to Joynelle Tucker, the high-school principal's wife.
The woman with the small sheets of tinfoil plastered all over her
head looked timidly around the corner. "We called 911 but we
never heard a siren." She was soon joined by a group of females
in various stages of the hairdressing process.

"What happened?" one of the ladies asked.

"Lord have mercy," Raylene said, putting a motherly arm
around Joynelle's shoulders. "Honey, we've got to get that stuff
out of your hair. It's gonna burn right up." She led Joynelle off
to wash out the highlighting bleach. "Mr. Win and Miss Kenni
took him right down. I swear, girl, I've never seen anything quite
like it." She emphasized her point with a giggle. "After they got
him down, I sat on him until Booty Carter got around to getting
his fat butt over here."

Her comment sent the ladies into a spate of giggles. And why
not? Successful termination of the fight-or-flight response generally had a euphoric effect.

"You did great," Toolie said, folding Kenni in a hug. "And,

you, handsome dog, I'd select you for my team any day of the week and twice on Sunday." She gave Win a wink.

"I second that," Mrs. Horatio declared, leading the rest of the ladies in a round of applause that was accompanied by catcalls, whistles and leers.

Win was used to receiving appreciative looks from ladies; however, this felt like a whole new ball game. He was afraid he had acquired a rabid fan club. Although if it got him invited to the garden party, that might not be such a bad thing.

"Do you know who that was?" The question came from Mrs. Laverne Hightower, an octogenarian and archivist of most of the town's secrets.

Win had a premonition her explanation would bowl him over. But he had to ask. "Who was it?"

Although Mrs. Hightower wasn't an inch over four foot ten she somehow managed to command the attention of a room full of overexcited women.

"He was that old fart Crumpy Hardaway's grandson." She emphasized her identification by slamming her hands on her skinny hips.

Win looked to Kenni; however, it was obvious from the look on her face that she was clueless.

"Who are you talking about?" Leave it to Raylene to get to the point.

Mrs. Hightower snorted. "Crumpy is the head of that clan of rednecks that lives out in the swamp. They've had their knickers in a twist about Miss Kenni's family since right after the war. My great-granny said they got to shootin' at each other over the deed to some land. Crumpy's kin thought they got the short end of the stick, and the families have been enemies ever since. Wouldn't surprise me none if those boys weren't trying to start somethin' again. They're pure white trash. They don't have the good sense God gave a cockroach."

"I've never heard anything about a Hatfield and McCoy feud involving my family," Kenni said. "What war are you talking about?"

"The War of Northern Aggression, of course."

"Of course," Kenni agreed with a grin. Only in the South could a family feud last over a century. "Okay, the excitement's over, so let's see if we can get this place back to normal."

"I have a great idea," Toolie said after she stopped shaking.

Kenni's friend was not at her best during a crisis. And this was by far worse than the time she overprocessed the preacher's wife's hair and it fell out in clumps. Remembering that event, and the stylist's somewhat unorthodox approach to the predicament, Kenni mentally did a big uh-oh. Toolie's ideas tended to be way, way, way out in left field.

"I think you should let Win use the apartment upstairs."

Oh, boy—Toolie wanted to give a homeless guy unlimited access to the building?

"Uh, well, uh…"

"I think it's a great idea," Raylene said. Darn, she'd always been a sucker for the bad-boy, hero type, and unfortunately, Win fit that description to a T.

"Yes, that would be lovely." Leave it to Mrs. Horatio to express an opinion.

"Oh, yeah," Joynelle agreed.

Kenni didn't concur with either sentiment, but she was delighted to notice that Joynelle's hair hadn't been burned to a bloody crisp.

"I don't think…" She started to say "that's a good idea," but before she could complete the thought she was interrupted by a chorus of support for her newest employee.

"All right, all right. But—" she turned to Mr. Gorgeous, who looked amazingly sheepish "—this is temporary. One month only. And, if I don't like you as a tenant, you're out of there. Are we in agreement?"

"Yes, ma'am."

Chapter Seven

Win couldn't believe his luck. Adios and good riddance to the Magnolia Inn. He had a place to live—goodbye, cockroaches, hello, clean bathroom. And best of all, no more audible trysts in the next room.

His new digs were definitely on the Spartan side. The bed looked lumpy, but it was private and it was his, at least for a while. And a while was all he needed because the minute he won the bet, he was history. Georgetown never looked more alluring.

Win unloaded his two sacks of newly purchased groceries. He was astonished at how tough it was to shop when you didn't have wheels. Oh well, he was now the proud owner of most of the basics—toilet paper, bread, fruit, coffee, peanut butter and beer. It was also amazing how expensive everything seemed when one suddenly morphed into a penny-pincher who would make Scrooge look generous. God, what he wouldn't give for just one of his credit cards.

It's only a month, it's only a month—and with that in mind, Win popped the top on one of his prize beers and leaned back to survey his kingdom. The Goodwill reject couch was scary and the toilet was cranky, but it was a port in a storm and all that nonsense.

CHAOS REIGNED when Win reported to work the next day. The phone was ringing off the wall, women were demanding entrance, and the salon wasn't even open.

"What's happening?" he asked his new boss. Boy, was she cute, even considering the scowl.

"This…this is happening." She made an all-encompassing motion with her arms and then shot him a look that could curdle milk.

It took a few moments for Win to process what she was talking about, and when he did he was astonished. The counters were loaded with baked goods—several plates of chocolate chip cookies, at least two pound cakes, pastries of every description, a big banana pudding-type thing, and even what looked like a pineapple upside-down cake.

"Did someone die?"

"No! Not unless you decide to kick the bucket," Kenni exclaimed before she stormed toward her office.

"What did I do?"

Raylene patted his hand. "Sugar, you didn't do a thing. Not a single thing. You're just the most handsome man to hit Magnolia Bluffs in a very long time."

"What?"

"This—" Raylene indicated the plethora of baked goods "—is a Southern girl's way of catching the eye of an eligible bachelor. And a few of these goodies came from overzealous mamas who want grandkids real bad."

"You have *got* to be kidding," Win exclaimed, barely able to keep his mouth from dropping open.

"Nope, I'm as serious as a speeding ticket. Right, Toolie?"

Toolie held a chocolate chip cookie in one hand and a peanut butter morsel in her other fist. "Damned straight. And may I say, keep up the good work."

The phone rang again, and Win discovered that as of yesterday afternoon, appointments at Permanently Yours were at a premium. It seemed that single women all over town were clamoring for a cut, curl or color.

KENNI WATCHED THE ACTION from the safety of her office. She noticed that once Win got over the surprise of the bakery barrage, he'd reverted to his own natural brand of charisma.

That man could charm the birds out of the trees. Fortunately she wasn't susceptible.

No way!

Animal magnetism aside, Kenni's female intuition was jumping up and down waving red flags. Sure he was alluring, and sexy, and too yummy for words, but there was also something fishy about him. He wasn't your run-of-the-mill underachiever; so why *was* he working in her salon?

And what *exactly* was he doing in Magnolia Bluffs? The first thing that came to mind was he was running from the law. However, since he didn't seem the least bit intimidated by Booty, he probably wasn't a fleeing felon. So that left—what? Getting the heck away from a vindictive wife. Trying to find his inner child? Get real!

The whole thing was giving her a headache. And the two dingbats who worked for her didn't help matters. Every time Win showed up, they turned into giggling loons.

Not that Kenni could blame them. Just the sight of Win Whittaker was enough to make a normal girl drool. And she was a one-hundred-percent normal American girl. He almost made her reassess her self-imposed celibacy.

Yikes! What *was* she thinking?

Chapter Eight

Quit ogling the hired help, it's not professional, Kenni thought as she scoped out his fine butt one last time. Women of all sizes and shapes were streaming into the salon demanding her staff's attention, and as much as she hated to do it, it was time for her to head into the fray.

The day went by in a whirl of cuts and color. Kenni couldn't remember ever being quite that busy. Win Whittaker was drawing in women like bees to honey. The last client had given him a suggestive up-and-down and slipped him her phone number before she'd sashayed out the door. Jeez!

Kenni plopped in her chair and waited for the last customer to leave. She was exhausted and she knew her employees were equally as tired.

Raylene fell onto the adjacent stool. "My puppies are woofin'," she announced, taking off her shoe and rubbing her foot. "I think we could use a bit of libation. How about it?"

Toolie had finally finished a complicated series of cornrows and joined them. "Lord, that makes my hands hurt," she proclaimed, shaking her fingers in an attempt to restore circulation. "And definitely, I want a libation, if that's anything like an alcoholic drink."

Fortunately or unfortunately, as the case may be, Raylene

kept a pitcher of margarita mix in the refrigerator. She said it was for emergencies, and they all agreed this qualified.

"Where's Mr. Sexy?" Raylene asked as she handed out plastic glasses of lime-green liquid.

"I think he went to his apartment," Kenni responded. "I wouldn't bet the farm on it, but I suspect he's not used to being around quite *that* many women."

"Can you blame him?" Toolie ended her question with a hoot of laughter. "They about drove me nuts, and I'm around them all the time."

"Now, to get back to business." Raylene took a big swig of margarita. "The wedding is coming up on Saturday, and you, missy—" she pointed at Kenni "—are dateless."

"Tell me something I don't already know." Kenni snorted in disgust. "I have the perfect outfit and no date. And despite my previous statements to the contrary, I do need an escort."

It was the first time she'd publicly admitted her deficiency. "But I'd have better luck finding gold at the end of a rainbow than digging up a suitable guy in Magnolia Bluffs."

"Ain't that the truth," Raylene agreed. "However, you cannot, repeat, *can not* go to that shindig without a man. Not when that mama's boy Walter Harrington is going to be the best man. We want him to rue the day he didn't stand up to that she-witch he calls a mother. It's called a woman's revenge. So, I have an idea."

God spare her from Raylene's ideas, especially if, as she suspected, it had something to do with Win Whittaker.

"We'll go back to Plan A, not that we have a Plan B."

Kenni was tired. Her feet hurt. Her head was pounding, and she really wasn't in the mood for one of Raylene's nutty schemes. Too bad she couldn't seem to control her mouth.

"Remind me what Plan A is."

Raylene was wearing a leer that didn't bode well for Kenni's frame of mind. "Plan A is Win. If you remember, that's how this whole thing got started. We saw him outside the window and discussed hiring him to take you to the wedding."

"No way."

"Oh, yes," Toolie squealed. "He's gorgeous, charming, and all the women love him."

"No."

"The jeans and T-shirt won't hack it, but we can get him all dressed up." By that time, Raylene was well into her I'll-take-charge mode and Toolie wasn't far behind.

"I said no." Talk about spitting in the wind.

"Harold works at the Haberdashery, and I've got enough on him that he'll do anything I want."

Harold was Raylene's second husband, or was he her third? Not that it mattered. At any rate, the Haberdashery was Magnolia Bluffs' version of an emporium of fine gentlemen's clothing.

"So?" Why couldn't she seem to formulate a cogent sentence?

"So, we'll get Harold to fix him up. I'm sure he can find something appropriate for us to 'borrow.'" Raylene scrunched her fingers and made quotation marks in the air. "And I personally think Mr. Sexy will clean up just fine."

So did Kenni, and therein was the problem. He was heart-stopping in a pair of old jeans and a T-shirt. What would he look like in a fancy suit? The image was enough to send her into a hot flash, and Lord in heaven, she was way too young for that kind of nonsense.

EVEN DURING HIS WORST DAY at court, Win had never experienced anything quite like his day at Permanently Yours—pandemonium, potential hearing loss, and last, but certainly not least, estrogen overload.

Win needed a cold brew and he was about to satisfy that desire when someone banged on his door. Considering he only knew three people in town, he was fairly sure he could identity his visitors, or visitor. If bad fortune hadn't been following him like a stray dog, he might get lucky and discover a certain cute little Georgia peach on the other side of the door.

But the chances of that were slim and none. She scowled at him every time she saw him. He opened the door to admit Toolie, Raylene and an obviously reluctant Kenni.

"Hey, ladies, come on in." Was his luck about to change?

Raylene and Toolie pranced in, claiming seats on the ratty couch. Kenni followed them and proceeded to prowl around the room.

Raylene was the first to speak. "We have a deal for you."

"A deal?" Win asked, turning a wooden kitchen chair around to straddle it.

The coconspirators on the couch leaned forward.

"It's a great opportunity." This time Toolie started the conversation.

"Kenni would like to give you a raise in return for an itsy, bitsy favor," she continued.

"Is that right?" Win glanced at the woman in question. She looked like she'd rather smooch a boa constrictor than continue the discussion.

Win didn't normally consider himself a perverse kind of guy, but this time he couldn't resist teasing her.

"Miss Kenni, what kind of itsy, bitsy favor would you like from me?" Itsy, bitsy? He hadn't heard that term in ages and he was positive he'd never used it.

Kenni ran her hand through her hair. "I, uh, I, hmm…"

"Spit it out, girl," Raylene demanded.

"I need a date for Saturday."

She said it so fast Win wasn't sure he'd heard her right.

"You want me to take you somewhere?"

Kenni heaved a deep sigh and plunked herself on the other end of the sofa. "Yes."

This was entertaining. Why would someone as attractive as

Kenni have to hire a date? As Win watched emotions flit across her face, he contemplated his current life in the slow lane. Especially high on his "think about" list was his delectable boss and the stupid bet he'd made with Colby.

But first things first, and the initial item on the agenda was Kenni McAllister—feisty, funny, blond, and extremely attractive. The problem was she wasn't his type. His style was someone who was professional, cool and elegant; not a woman who elicited thoughts of baby car seats and big shaggy dogs. And did he mention vivid images of hot, sweaty sex?

Wait a minute. She said date, not marriage.

KENNI WAS PRAYING that the floor would open up and swallow her. In the annals of embarrassing moments, this one had to be a new low. Not only was it humiliating, it was downright tacky. It took a few minutes to coordinate her mouth and brain, but she finally managed it and took over the explanation.

"It's like this." That was how she started her description of the wedding, her relationship with Walter and her current conundrum.

Chapter Nine

The guy was unbelievable in a pair of faded jeans, but holy catfish, that hadn't prepared her for the sight of Win in an expensive suit and a crisp white shirt. It didn't take more than three seconds for Kenni's initial rush of erotic thoughts to be diluted by Harold's clucky, mother-hen routine.

"Don't spill anything on the suit that I can't get out by dry-cleaning," Raylene's ex demanded as he nitpicked Win's entire ensemble.

"Okay, sure. And don't wipe my face with the tie, right?"

Win's reply was sarcasm at its best. Kenni was surprised he hadn't smacked the nervous haberdasher upside the head with the tie.

"You kids have fun," Raylene said, shooing them out the door.

"You're not my mother and this isn't the prom," Kenni snapped. Kenni just couldn't help herself. Sometimes her friend was simply too much to take. She wouldn't even be going to this wedding if the bride wasn't Uncle Dave's second cousin twice removed. And skipping a family shindig simply wasn't done.

"Here." Kenni threw her car keys to Win. "You do have a driver's license, don't you?" She hated being a shrew, but this scenario was bringing out the worst in her.

"Yes, ma'am," her date replied, gracing her with a smile that could melt the hardest heart, and hers wasn't made of tempered steel. Not by a long shot.

THE CEREMONY was short but Kenni was afraid the reception would be interminable. The Magnolia Bluffs Country Club was awash in a sea of white satin, pastel roses and twinkle lights. If her stomach hadn't felt as if it were being assaulted by an army of gastric gnomes, Kenni would have thought the place was a fairyland. In reality—especially considering her ex was flirting with some nubile debutante that even his mother could love— Kenni felt as if she were entering a prelude to purgatory.

"Would you like a drink?" Win asked.

Not only did he clean up like a champ, he had the manners of a gentleman. And that led to more suspicion about his background and motivation. He was no more a drifter than Kenni was a pole dancer.

"Champagne?" Win retrieved two flutes from the tray of a passing waiter. He was obviously used to taking charge. Could he be a CIA spy? Darn, she was getting nutty again.

"I'll bet we could find a strawberry or two if we looked around," he murmured, leaning over to nuzzle her neck.

Had they turned the air conditioner off, or was it just her? Kenni thought about ditching the jacket to her perfect outfit, but that would ruin the look she'd worked so hard to achieve.

Why *had* she spent so much time shopping? Oh, right. She wanted to impress Walter. And why did she want to do that?

She surreptitiously studied her ex-husband and tried to remember what it was that had attracted her in the first place. Time had taken its toll. Beside the fact he was about as deep as a kiddie pool, he was also going to seed. Even though they lived in the same town Kenni made sure they rarely ran into each other. So when she did see him she was always surprised at his appearance.

"Did I tell you how beautiful you look?" Win's softly asked question jerked her out of her reverie. The intimate male voice sent goose bumps up and down Kenni's spine. Holy Batman!

Anna Belle and Eugenie had served up good manners with the Frosted Flakes, so it was time to drag them out, dust them off, and use them. "Thank you, that was very kind."

"Kindness has nothing to do with it," he murmured, placing his hand at the small of her back. "Would you like to wander over to the buffet and then find a table?"

Food, table—yep, that would work. "Sure. In fact, I see my cousin Liza over there. Let's join her." Kenni wasn't quite sure how Liza and Maizie would react to her date; however, she knew she was about to find out. Her two favorite relatives rarely ever pulled their punches.

"Hey, Liza, are you saving those seats?" Kenni asked. Her cousin responded by pulling her into a hug.

"Just for you and…" Liza waved a hand in Win's direction, giving him a thorough survey in the process. "Maizie and I have been looking everywhere for you."

"This is my date, Win Whittaker. Win, this my cousin Liza Henderson and her friend Charlie Taylor." Liza's husband had suddenly died of a heart attack at age thirty-eight. Charlie was her business partner and one of her best buddies.

The two men shook hands and when Liza extended hers in greeting, Win made the surprise move of kissing it instead.

Kenni wasn't sure what that was all about, but the look on her cousin's face was priceless. It wasn't often Liza was rendered speechless.

"Sweetie, who *is* this marvelous specimen?" That honeyed drawl could belong only to Maizie.

As Kenni made the appropriate introductions, she surreptitiously checked out the table settings. Big problem. There were forks of every shape, size and description. She was an honors graduate from Miss Alicia's School of Etiquette, and she still didn't recognize half of the utensils.

She really didn't want Win to be embarrassed. Maybe she could give him a few subtle hints. Her misgivings, however, were totally unfounded.

Who was he?

"What did you say you do for a living?" That question came from Maizie's husband, Clayton, otherwise known as Clay. Kenni couldn't wait to hear the answer.

"I'm having a sort of temporary career change," Win answered.

Obviously not satisfied with that information, Clay persevered. "From what to what?"

Kenni's family was very protective. Sometimes that proved to be useful. At other times, it was simply aggravating.

"I work for Ms. McAllister right now. When I return to Virginia, I'll go back to a little business my partner and I have."

Kenni hoped to goodness that "little business" didn't involve the wrong side of the law.

"What kind of business?" Clay persisted. Everyone at the table waited intently for Win's answer.

"I deal with the criminal justice system."

Kenni's heart took a nosedive. She was right; he *was* too good to be true. He was gorgeous, funny, brave, and probably wanted by the law.

Damn it!

The interrogation was cut short when Holly Horatio—Viola's only heir and a bimbo extraordinaire—barreled up. The fact she was missing a few brain cells was negated by the small detail that she had a body reminiscent of Carmen Electra. And even more unfortunate, she was accompanied by Walter.

"Well, hello there," Holly gushed, practically pushing Kenni out of the way. "Mother told me all about you," she said to Win. "I would have welcomed you sooner but I don't get my hair done *here.* I go to Atlanta. Do you like it?" she asked, suggestively weaving her fingers through her highlighted locks.

Kenni had no doubt Holly had paid a fortune for that over-processed mess. She was so busy thinking catty thoughts she forgot Walter was standing beside her.

When he spoke to Liza, Kenni suddenly had the epiphany that her ex had always blended into the woodwork, and that even without his mother's influence, they never would have stayed together.

Walter's personality was eclipsed by his strong-willed mother, while Kenni yearned for someone who made her skin tingle and her heart palpitate. That certainly didn't describe Walter. It was sad but true; theirs hadn't been a match made in heaven.

"Hello, Kenni." Walter finally acknowledged her presence. "You look very nice," he said.

Nice! Nice! She'd worked damned hard to make him rue the day he dumped her; and all he said was she looked *nice.* What had happened to the stab of lust, or at the very least the drool she'd hoped to achieve? As much as Kenni hated to admit defeat, it wasn't going to happen. Walter's mother wouldn't think it was seemly.

"Are you all right?" Win asked, putting his arm around her waist.

"I'm fine," Kenni assured him, hoping against hope that he'd drop the subject. She really didn't want to discuss her marriage, or Walter, or anything else that was vaguely personal.

Bless her heart, Holly demanded his attention. "So, Mother said she baked a batch of brownies for you, seeing as how you were so courageous, and all. My mother makes the best brownies in town. Don't ya think?"

Win's expression didn't reveal a thing. Was he buying into the bimbo's spiel or not?

"Let's dance." Holly practically yanked him out of his chair.

"Don't worry," Liza remarked as Holly steamrolled Win toward the dance floor. "I don't know the guy. But I'm sure he has more sense than to be taken in by that tart."

Charlie and Clay chuckled. And as a result of his nonverbal contribution to the conversation, Maizie's husband received an admonition. "Watch yourself."

"Yes, sweetie," Clay replied. Then both men laughed again.

"I'm gonna invite Mr. Whittaker to Sunday dinner. That will give us a chance to grill him properly," Liza announced. Her sister nodded in agreement. They might not look alike, but it sometimes seemed like they worked with a single mind.

"No, you're not," Kenni exclaimed. "He doesn't mean anything to me, so why would you want to ask him over. That seems so…so intimate, especially considering he's a stranger. I've only known him two weeks."

"That's precisely why we're going to invite him. If he plans to hang out with our favorite relative, we want the straight skinny on him."

Oh, boy! Just butter her butt and call her a biscuit.

Chapter Ten

True to their word, Liza and Maizie issued an invitation that Win couldn't resist. So there they were, one big happy family doing Sunday dinner. Au contraire! It was more like the Spanish Inquisition than a friendly meal.

And astonishing as it might seem, the family had lost almost all the battles in this war of wills. Win had more moves than Jerry Rice.

"Is this anything like your mama's fried chicken recipe?" Anna Belle asked.

She was good. No wonder—her skills had been honed from years of dealing with fifth graders.

"No, ma'am. My mother never was much of a cook. But this is wonderful. My compliments to the chef," he said with a grin.

Kenni had to admit that he knew the perfect path to a Southern woman's heart.

Win Whittaker was slick as grease owl spit—much too smooth for Kenni's taste.

Yeah, right!

She watched in awe as both Cora, their longtime housekeeper, and Anna Belle turned pink. Cora had to be at least eighty but she still knew her way around a kitchen, and apparently she wasn't immune to a compliment.

And Anna Belle—what could you say about Anna Belle

Carpenter Nunn, other than she was a firecracker. After she
retired from teaching, she went straight into activism and then
segued to politics and the city council.

"Have you decided whether you're going to run for mayor?"
Kenni asked. She had a few tricks up her sleeve, and engaging
Anna Belle, Eugenie and Sheriff Dave in a discussion of local
government was the easiest way she knew to change the subject.
Win obviously realized what she was doing and sent her a smile
of gratitude.

Her little trick, however, didn't deter her determined cousins.

"So, did I hear you say you were from Virginia? I had a
sorority sister from McLean. Is that anywhere near your home?"
Maizie asked.

Kenni whacked her on the shin; however, it didn't stop her for
more than a second. She was a woman on a mission.

Win gave her one of the smiles that Kenni was starting to think
of as his cat-in-the-creamery grins.

"I grew up in Loudon County," he replied. "But, I don't live
there now."

"Where *do* you live?" Clay asked. Maizie had unobtrusively
managed to lob the conversational ball to her husband.

There was the grin again. "I live here."

In a skirmish of wits, Win had to be declared the winner.

Clay had the good grace to laugh. "I know when I'm beat. So
what do you think about those Braves? Think they can win the
pennant this year?"

Fortunately, Win had a working knowledge of baseball, and
no matter how hard the sisters tried to derail the sports conversation, even *they* couldn't breach the brotherhood of the bull
pen.

So Sunday dinner progressed. The cuisine was a surefire contender for the comfort food hall of fame.

"I hope you left room for some peach cobbler and homemade ice cream." Anna Belle stood to collect the dishes.

"Give me about thirty minutes and I'll be ready," Win said with a laugh. "Why don't you sit down and let us clean up." He took the stack of plates out of her hand.

If he kept that up, her family would adopt him, and that would make him her brother. Aargh!

Win suppressed a grin. Kenni's relatives were not only delightful, they were nosy as all get-out. Although he didn't know them well, he suspected Liza and Maizie wouldn't go down without a fight, and if he wasn't careful, they would eventually manage to trip him up.

"That was delicious," Win declared, barely resisting the urge to rub his stomach. After the younger members of the party cleaned the kitchen, they adjourned to the sunporch for coffee and sweets.

It didn't take a rocket scientist to realize that the minute the cobbler was put away, the questions would recommence. Fortunately, Kenni had other ideas.

"I understand the mayor was caught crawling around under Miss Dolly's shrubbery," she commented, almost too casually.

He could tell by her subtle smirk that she knew exactly what she was doing. She was so cute he couldn't resist giving her hand a gentle squeeze.

Sheriff Dave choked on his coffee, and Anna Belle gave an unladylike guffaw.

"That twit can't keep his zipper up. He thinks every woman in town is just waiting for him. Delusional old goat." Maizie wasn't at all reticent about describing the politician's proclivities.

Smart guy that he was, Dave nodded, but remained silent.

Anna Belle didn't feel compelled to follow suit. "Miss Dolly wouldn't spit on the geezer if he was on fire."

In the ensuing discussion Win discovered that Miss Dolly was the estranged wife of Harold Trout, the president of the city council. And the police had been involved in several skirmishes involving the trio. Writers for the soap operas would have a field day with this one.

"I talked to him after my deputy found him with mud all over his knees. He claims he was looking for his dog." Dave laughed as he joined the discussion. "The problem is he doesn't have a pooch. Even dogs can't stand him."

"The rumor is that Harold cornered the old fool at the Kiwanis meeting and threatened to beat the stuffin' out of him if he didn't straighten up and fly right." Anna Belle gave a huff and settled back on the wicker settee. "If the mayor doesn't watch out, I'm gonna help Harold." She negated her threat with a giggle.

"However, I plan to be a bit more devious. I'm going to personally make sure he gets voted out of office," she admitted.

"I heard at the salon that Harold's taken to packin' a gun," Kenni said, then leaned back to wait for the blowup.

"Lord have mercy!" Eugenie exclaimed. "Those two old men are as blind as bats. We can't have someone getting shot at a council meeting. What can you do about it, Dave?"

"I really don't want to hear any of this," the sheriff said, scratching his head. Then he sighed in resignation. "I'll send a deputy to the next meeting. Do you think that'll help?" He addressed his question to Anna Belle.

"I sure hope so. We haven't had a murder in Magnolia Bluffs in at least ten years. We don't want one now, especially not if it involves a couple of our esteemed city fathers."

TEN YEARS! A murder happened every ten minutes in D.C. Win marveled at the ultimate in cultural disconnect. Maybe taking some time away from murder and mayhem *would* be good for his soul.

Anything permanent would put a huge crimp in his income. Plus, leaving his practice would be a gigantic lifestyle change. Where had *that* idea come from? He would *never* consider doing anything that drastic. Would he?

As much as he hated to admit it, the relaxed atmosphere of Magnolia Bluffs was appealing.

Chapter Eleven

Kenni was enjoying a Monday-morning coffee with Liza when her cousin tossed in a conversational grenade. "A thank-you note? Win sat down and wrote Anna Belle a note, on paper, with a pen? And he delivered it." That did it—the guy was definitely not homeless, nor was he down on his luck. So exactly what was he doing in Magnolia Bluffs? And why had he been holding her hand at dinner? Not that she minded. No indeedy!

"Yes, ma'am. And just to throw in my two cents' worth, I think he's a mighty handsome man," Liza announced.

So did Kenni, but she wasn't about to admit that to her cousin. No way. There wasn't a man alive she'd let under her skin, even if he was the most appealing person she'd ever known. It was that once-burned-twice-shy stuff.

"You invited me to coffee so you could tell me Win has manners?"

"No, you dummy. Maizie and I want you to know we're giving him our seal of approval. We're not sure about his employment situation but we think he has potential."

THE NEXT DAY Kenni was still pondering the Win situation, when the object of her ruminations strolled in the back door. The salon was closed on Mondays so she hadn't seen him since their infamous Sunday dinner.

Kenni couldn't decide whether to play it cool or be totally mortified. Unfortunately, her family hadn't been very subtle in their questioning, and they'd been even less circumspect in bestowing their endorsement.

Darn their hides.

All things considered—pushy relatives, resorting to hiring a date, etcetera, etcetera—he must think she was the biggest wall-flower in central Georgia. And considering the fact her love life was virtually nonexistent, she probably was. The pity party had to stop. Right this minute!

He was handsome, fun, and apparently had a working knowl-edge of Miss Manners. Add it all up, and her renegade heart lapsed into wishful thinking. That had to come to an end as well.

Something wasn't quite right about him, and as hard as she tried, Kenni couldn't figure out what it was. One thing for certain; he was as out of his element in a beauty salon as a preacher in a bordello.

KENNI'S FAMILY WAS a hoot, and Liza and Maizie had missed their calling. Their interrogation skills would put Nancy Grace to shame. Even the wedding had been entertaining, and Win wasn't a big fan of nuptials. It seemed like saying "I do" was a prelude to disaster. Or was that just the cynic in him talking.

Maybe his life in the fast lane wasn't all it was cracked up to be. In a rare moment of doubt, Win had second thoughts about his chosen lifestyle. Would it be feasible to live and work some-where other than D.C.?

No way!

Why not? That was a question he couldn't answer.

"Hey, Mr. Win. How ya doin'?" The friendly greeting came from Kenni's janitor, Bubba Gene Guthrie.

"Not bad, Bubba Gene, not bad at all."

Shortly after Win started work at Permanently Yours, Raylene had told the story about Bubba Gene, and Kenni's campaign to help him become a functioning member of society.

The gentle giant, with the IQ of a small child, had lived with his mother his entire life. When Mrs. Guthrie died, he was set adrift. That is, until Kenni gave him a job at the salon. Not only did she trust Bubba Gene to work as her janitor, she cajoled, bribed and charmed several friends into hiring him as their gardener.

And if adoring looks were any indication, Bubba Gene would do anything for his boss and friend.

"Did you have a nice weekend?" Win asked.

"Yes, sir, I shor' did. That movie I'm partial to was at the Grand on Saturday." He hitched up his overalls and scratched his belly. "You know the one with uh…uh…Raylene, what's her name?"

Raylene was preparing her station for the upcoming day. "Ariel," she replied without looking up. "He's talking about *The Little Mermaid*," she explained to Win.

He shook his head, understanding everything. "Oh, okay. Hey, Bubba, I'm glad you enjoyed yourself."

"Yes, sir. I even had enough money to buy popcorn," Bubba Gene said as he continued to sweep, humming as he worked.

Win watched the janitor for a few moments. In Magnolia Bluffs it was possible to be happy with few material possessions. In his world, a guy could get killed for his sneakers.

Perhaps there was something to be said for the Southern way of life; not that he was really considering staying. Or to paraphrase Bubba Gene, "No, sirree."

Win had barely wiped the grin from his face when his incredibly attractive boss stomped toward the back of the salon.

Yep, she stomped. Or at the least she made as much racket as someone who didn't weigh more a hundred pounds soakin' wet could make. Oops! Did he really drop that *g?* And was speaking Southern catching?

"Here." She poked a plate at him, forcing him to bend over to prevent being maimed.

"What's this?" he asked, holding up a platter of baked goods.

"It's a coconut cake. Holly Horatio left it for you. Eat it quick or we'll get ants, and I sure don't want to have to call the exterminator," she announced before marching off.

"Our boss lady doesn't look too happy," Raylene said, grinning ear to ear as she continued to get ready for the onslaught of clients.

He tried to hand her the cake. "Would you like this?"

"Not me. I don't like coconut."

Win suspected it was more like she didn't like Holly Horatio, but he kept his mouth shut. He was a smart guy, and he had an Ivy League education to prove it.

"I'll take it," Bubba Gene said, leaning on his broom. "Mama used to make me those. She's gone now, ya know."

Win didn't know how to respond so he simply handed over the cake.

Bubba Gene wandered off with a smile plastered on his face.

"You made his day, ya know that? I just hope Holly didn't mix up the salt and sugar. She's not exactly the brightest gal around."

Win had already figured that out so he didn't bother to answer.

"Uh-oh. Here comes another one of your admirers." Raylene nodded in the direction of the front desk. "And it looks like she's bearing gifts."

Win barely managed to keep a straight face as a slightly chubby woman carrying a tin of cookies barreled his way. She would have been attractive if her hair hadn't been a weird shade of olive-green.

Win looked to Toolie for guidance; this was her client, but she grinned and continued to putter around her station.

Prior to his gig at Permanently Yours, Win's only experience with beauty salons had been periodic haircut appointments. After two weeks at the salon, he had a new appreciation for the profession. The staff heard more sob stories than a bartender.

"Here you go." The woman shoved an improvised tinfoil plate at him. "Cookies. Peanut butter. I hope you're not allergic to peanuts. You should call my niece. She plays the piano." The woman didn't wait for him to reply before she picked up a strand of hair and waved it at Toolie.

"Toolie, you've got to help me," she wailed.

No kidding!

"Win, would you please give Charlene a nice relaxing shampoo." Toolie ended her request with an expression that could only be interpreted as a cross between a smirk and a wink.

"Charlene, sweetie, you pop yourself right over to the shampoo bowl. Win will take care of you. And why don't you tell him how you got yourself into that fix?"

His frown elicited a giggle.

Win ushered the distraught woman over to the sink and managed to get her settled before she started her story.

"I have an invitation to this great wedding next weekend. The reception is going to be at the Atlanta Country Club," she gushed. "Can you believe it? My cousin's cousin is taking me as his date. So naturally, I wanted to look my best. And I was getting some gray so I did the color myself. I don't know what happened. I hope to goodness Toolie can fix it."

So did Win, but he was too smart to voice his misgivings. That was just the beginning of the woman's chatter. It was enough to drive a sane man crazy.

The next client was a brunette he hadn't met before. She was prim, proper and so uptight she looked like she was about to snap. Something about her reminded Win of all the English teachers he'd had in high school.

But the good news was, she didn't look like she'd ever baked a cookie.

His illusion of safety evaporated like mist on a hot day when he glanced at Raylene. She was laughing her head off—obviously at his expense.

What now?

It didn't take Win long to figure it out. The brunette *really* enjoyed a good shampoo. The more Win massaged her scalp, the louder she got.

"Ooh, ooh, aaah. Oh, yes." Shades of Meg Ryan in *When Harry Met Sally!*

"You are dead meat," he mouthed to Raylene. She responded with a belly laugh.

THAT WAS ONLY THE BEGINNING of the day. They had a parade of senior citizens sporting corkscrew purple perms, housewives who thought they needed a trim and a couple of teenagers who wanted cornrows. The seniors and housewives were not only bearing goodies for Win, they were also armed with names and phone numbers of cousins, aunts, friends and one woman even brought the number of a checker from the Piggly Wiggly. The front counter looked like a bake sale at the Baptist church.

The last client was paying her bill when Win adjourned to the back of the salon. He'd seen enough hair to last him a lifetime, and he'd had his butt grabbed more than once.

"I have to apologize," Kenni said. He hadn't heard her come in, but there she was in all her pixie glory. She'd had a hard day and she was still as cute and luscious as a Georgia peach.

Funny thing, he'd never had libidinous thoughts about cute before. His previous women had all been glamorous. In fact he'd never harbored ideas of permanent before, and with this woman, that's all he seemed to be contemplating. *That* had to come to a halt. Immediately, if not sooner!

Win's only goal was to win the bet and then get back to his

law practice, post haste. When in doubt he always went with the old saying, better the devil you know. And this Georgia "devil" was a total enigma. Not that he thought Kenni was evil—no indeed! And therein was the problem.

"What are you apologizing for, peaches?"

"For that whole coconut cake debacle." She waved a hand in the air, somehow managing to look chagrined and sly at the same time. It was a cool trick if you could pull it off—and she managed. "Did you call me peaches?"

"No apology necessary, and yes, I did," Win admitted with a grin. He wondered if her pique was motivated by jealousy. Holly Horatio, Carmen Electra—yep, he strongly suspected Kenni had met the green-eyed monster. She liked him. Hot damn!

"I'm starving. Could I talk you into going to dinner with me?" he asked.

Kenni perused the array of baked goods before she raised an eyebrow.

"I need something containing protein," he said.

"Right. I can't believe I'm saying this but I am tired of banana nut bread. If this silly baking contest continues much longer, I'm gonna weigh three hundred pounds. Lord in heaven, the women in this town are acting like twits. You'd think they'd never seen a good-looking guy before."

"Good-looking, huh?" Win couldn't resist another grin.

"Don't let it go to your head. Most of them watch pro wrestling."

"Don't knock it. The WWE guys are ripped."

Kenni gave him one of her "whatever" looks and changed the subject. "What did you think of Cora Rutherford?"

Although Win was normally good with names, he was getting the clients at Permanently Yours all mixed up.

"You'll have to remind me which one she was."

"She's the brunette who equates a shampoo with, uh…"

Kenni broke into a huge laugh but eventually managed to finish her description. "Let's just say it's a little more intense for her than most people."

"Oh, yeah. She'd be hard to forget. Does that kind of thing happen often?" God, he hoped not!

Chapter Twelve

The Magnolia Bluffs Diner was known throughout the county for its gut-busting chili dogs (with onions and cheese), greasy cheeseburgers and calorie-laden milkshakes. The dinner fare was cholesterol at its best, and Win loved it. D.C. dining was not known for comfort cuisine. Sometimes in the fray of everyday life, he forgot that fusion was not the norm across a great portion of the country.

"Did you like your dinner?" Kenni gave his clean plate a significant look. "What have you been eating lately?"

Win hated to admit his diet had leaned heavily toward peanut butter sandwiches, Cheerios and cheap beer—with an occasional bologna sandwich thrown in for variety. "Not much good stuff. Dinner was delicious. Would you like some dessert?"

"No, I don't think so. If you get a hankering for some sweets just go back to the salon and take whatever you want. Please, take it all. I don't need the calories." Although his apartment key worked on both doors, Win wasn't comfortable wandering around the salon after hours.

"I've been promoted, haven't I?"

"Yes," she said with a smile.

"Cool. I'm stuffed. Can I talk you into going for a walk?"

"Uh-huh. A walk sounds good. I love summer evenings. That's when it gets cool and all the little critters come out to play."

Win had never actually pondered the nightlife of small animals, and calling the temperature cool was a bit of an overstatement.

IT SEEMED NATURAL for Win to take her hand as they strolled down the boulevard lined with towering magnolias. The fragrant scent of honeysuckle tickled Kenni's nose, bringing back good memories of her childhood. Crickets chirped their delight that the day had turned into evening. The old-fashioned streetlamps illuminated the sidewalk, giving the street the feeling of another time and place.

In Magnolia Bluffs, the period between dusk and dark was the time when children played hide-and-seek in the yard and collected fireflies to be kept overnight in a Mason jar. Although life had changed considerably in the past twenty years, there were some traditions, especially in a small Georgia town, that remained static. It all led to a feeling of permanence.

Adding to her enjoyment of the evening was the fact she was holding hands with a handsome man who seemed to want nothing more than her company. That hadn't been the case with Walter.

Stop that! Kenni shook all thoughts of her ex-husband from her mind. He was part of her past, not her present.

"Who's this?" Win asked as he pulled her to a stop in front of the statue of a Confederate general.

"That's General Joe Johnston."

"He's famous?"

"Yep. He was one of the best generals of the Confederacy, but he pissed off the president and got fired."

"Oops."

"Yeah, oops."

Win chuckled, and then sat down on the concrete bench at Joe's feet. He took her hand, silently urging her to join him.

"Let's talk."

Under ordinary circumstances, Kenni would have been tempted to break into chuckles. Imagine that—a man who wanted to talk. It was especially interesting considering that this one harbored more secrets than the Atomic Energy Commission.

"Okay," she agreed, joining him on the bench. Curiosity overrode her protective instinct.

"This is nice," he murmured, leaning back.

"Yes, it is, isn't it?" She was about to get comfortable when he threw her a curve ball.

"Why don't you tell me about your ex-husband?"

"My what?"

"Your ex. I've been wondering about him ever since the wedding. Being around him upsets you, doesn't it?"

Kenni pondered the question briefly and then decided to reply. Considering she had bribed Win into accompanying her to the wedding, she owed him an explanation.

"His name is Walter, but you know that. What else can I say about him? He's not one of my favorite people."

"That was loud and clear."

"Did I tell you I used to be a schoolteacher?"

"No, you didn't." Win sat up as if he was really interested in the rest of the story.

"Yes. English. Anyway, after I graduated from the University of Georgia I came home and immediately got a job at the high school. The fact that they hired me after a ten-minute interview should've been a huge red flag, or an omen of things to come." Kenni started to shrug, but ended up grinning. "His mother was on the school board. I needed a job. I had a brand-new degree and I was thrilled." She did another "whatever" motion with her hands.

"Walter was working at his mother's real estate office. We met at church and fell in love." Kenni verbally emphasized the *L* word. "At least I thought we were in love. In reality, he was in lust, and I was simply stupid."

"That sounds familiar. I have several divorced friends."

"We were happy for all of about, oh say, thirty-three seconds. Walter is a mama's boy. Are you familiar with that interesting character flaw?"

"Not really."

"Let me tell you, it's a killer in a marriage. His mother had access to our checking account even after we were married." Kenni shook her head. "She had a key to our house and would come over at all hours of the day and night. But the worst thing was she started following me. And Walter didn't do squat. She'd say 'jump,' and he'd reply, 'how high?' However, I probably would have stayed married to him if he hadn't issued an ultimatum."

"He had the guts to give you an ultimatum?"

"Yep. After a couple of years teaching and dealing with Beatrice Harrington, I knew that our marriage wasn't destined to last." Kenni chuckled. "My nickname for her was Beatrice the Beast. Guess that didn't help, huh? Anyway, Permanently Yours came on the market so I took money from my small trust fund and put a down payment on the salon. Then, I quit my job and went to cosmetology school. I knew I'd make more owning the salon than I could as a teacher. Plus, I'd finally realized that teaching wasn't what I wanted to do."

"And?"

"Walter's mother didn't think it was acceptable to have a beautician for a daughter-in-law, so he told me he'd divorce me if I didn't ditch my stupid idea. Dear old mom never thought I was good enough for her baby boy, especially since I started life in a trailer park. To put it mildly, snobbery was her strong suit."

"That's tough, especially in a town this small."

"It certainly was. The ironic thing is I suspect Walter will eventually try to get out from under her wing. And when he does, I'm afraid he's going to do something weird. It's not that I dislike him as much as I feel sorry for him."

Win responded with a shrug.

"So turnabout is fair play. How about you?" Kenni smiled at him.

"How about me what?"

"Do you have a wife, a girlfriend, a whatever?"

"I've never been married, and as far as girlfriends go, yeah, there have been some."

"Any serious ones?"

"You certainly are nosy." Win tempered his comment with a grin.

"What can I say," Kenni agreed. "I told you everything about my Walter experience, pitiful as it was. Now it's your turn."

Win casually put his arm on the bench behind her. "A while back I decided it was time to settle down, so I started dating a woman named Amelie. Looking back, I suppose I picked her because our families have been friends for years and it seemed like an easy solution. Was that ever a big mistake. She got so clingy I thought I was being smothered."

"She sounds kind of like kudzu."

Win grinned at her analogy. "Like kudzu. At any rate, I'm afraid I didn't do a very good job of breaking up because she calls me periodically or drops by my house."

Okay, maybe he was running from a bad girlfriend. That would be better than fleeing the law.

Then Kenni's curiosity got the best of her good manners. "Is she pretty?"

"Do you mean Amelie?" Win asked with a chuckle.

Kenni nodded, feeling like a jealous nitwit. What did she have to feel jealous about?

"Yes, she's pretty," Win said, running his finger down her cheek. "And that's enough discussion of Amelie. Tell me about Kenni McAllister's life."

Kenni then told him the story of her mother's death and the Carpenter sisters adopting her.

Win didn't say a word, so Kenni continued. "I have one last

comment about Walter. Neither he nor his mother intended to do anything nice for me, but in reality they did me the biggest favor in the world. They rocked me out of my complacency, and voila, I'm now the ex-Mrs. Walter Harrington and loving it. I consider my success a sweet revenge."

Win understood the concept of revenge. In his profession, he saw it every day. However, in his experience it usually included the use of a .357 Magnum. Things were very different in Magnolia Bluffs.

He was about to kiss her. And kiss her. And kiss her. And if there was a God in the heavens, Kenni would reciprocate. Please, God, let her reciprocate.

HE'S GONNA KISS ME. Oh, my word, he's gonna kiss me. That was Kenni's last rational thought before Win pulled her into his arms and touched his lips to hers. Their first kiss started out gently. It was perfect for a Southern night bathed in the glow of moonlight. It took him mere minutes to elevate the exploration of her mouth from innocent to sensuous.

Ooh la la.

Kenni barely had time for her brain to process the signals her nerve endings were sending, before he pulled back and rested his forehead on hers.

"That was, uh, that was great."

Was it ever!

"I think I should walk you home now."

That was *not* what she wanted to hear.

"Um, okay." On a scale of one to ten, Kenni's enthusiasm for strolling home rated somewhere close to a one-minus. More kissing—that rated an eight or nine—never mind they were in a public place.

"I live a couple of blocks in that direction." She indicated a tree-lined street leading away from the town square.

Much to Kenni's delight, Win pulled her to her feet and drew her into his arms. But best of all, he planted little butterfly kisses all over her face and neck.

Merciful heavens, did General Joe Johnston actually wink at her?

Chapter Thirteen

The next morning, Win was still reeling from the Kenni encounter that his libido had labeled THE KISS. Yep, he was definitely thinking in capital letters, and *that* made him extremely nervous.

Win's face had been on the cover of several magazines as one of D.C.'s most eligible bachelors. He'd also had more than his share of girlfriends, women whose attributes spanned the spectrum from gorgeous bodies, to highly-educated minds, to vibrant personalities. But thinking about Kenni conjured visions of a white bungalow with green shutters, a porch swing and a calico cat.

Whoa! That was an exact description of her house. The thought slammed him back into reality. Even if he could manage to fit into her life, would she ever be able to forgive his duplicity? Hell, no! She was a firecracker, and he was nothing but a con man and a liar. And the whole situation had come about because of a stupid bet.

So how was he going to dig himself out of his self-imposed hole? Win was contemplating the situation when Toolie groaned.

"Anything I can help you with?" He thought he'd make the offer even though he barely knew the difference between a henna and a highlight.

"No, Winnie Thompson wants me to redo her perm. She claims it's not tight enough. Merciful Pete, that hair of hers is tighter than poodle curls. She constantly wants a redo for something or other." Toolie slammed the appointment book shut and marched over to prepare for her customers, including the infamous Winnie Thompson.

So far, Kenni hadn't appeared. That was unusual since she normally opened the shop. Not that Win was getting worried, but it wasn't like her to be late.

"Hey, Raylene. Does Kenni have an appointment this morning?"

"Not that I know of." Raylene frowned. "I wonder where she is?"

That was a good question. But, Win wasn't her boyfriend or her daddy, and definitely not her keeper. She certainly wasn't obliged to share her schedule with him.

In lieu of breakfast, Win grabbed a fresh banana nut muffin. The flow of baked goods had abated, more than likely because he hadn't shown any interest in dipping into Magnolia Bluff's dating pool.

After devouring the first ten or twelve dozen cookies, he'd decided the chocolate chip should be the state delicacy of Georgia. The small delicacies came in every shape, size and convolution—featuring chunks, chips, oatmeal, raisins, hunks of candy bars and even peanut butter. But shouldn't those be called peanut-butter cookies?

Win was pondering the peanut thing almost as seriously as he would a tricky criminal defense. That's when realization hit him like a brick. It was time to ditch the bet, graciously set his partner up with his sister, and get the heck out of Magnolia Bluffs. If he didn't make an escape soon, his brain would curdle like cottage cheese. Was there something in the water that was making him crazy?

The entire time he was shampooing Betty Sue Hilliard, he was pondering water pollution. Thank God, she was one of the quiet ones. He had just completed her final rinse when he heard a loud noise up front.

What now?

Unfortunately, this "what now" ended up being worse than all of the other events—including the overload of chocolate chip cookies and the aborted robbery.

"Raylene, what are we going to do?" Kenni was hysterically waving the portable phone in the air.

Win took the receiver out of her hands. "Sweetheart, what's wrong?" he asked, drawing her into his arms.

He didn't miss the look Raylene shot him. She'd caught the "sweetheart" remark but Kenni obviously hadn't. Her answer was to burrow her face in his T-shirt and let go with a fresh surge of tears.

An audience had gathered and Win looked to the ladies for guidance. The unison of shrugs indicated he was on his own.

"Kenni, sweetheart. Look at me." He cupped her chin and lifted her face. "Tell me the problem. Maybe I can help."

She swiped at her face like a small child. "I don't think you can do anything. Not unless you're some kind of Perry Mason."

That hit closer to home than he was willing to admit.

"What do you mean?"

"Bubba Gene's been arrested for murder."

The ladies reacted in unison.

"What?" Raylene squealed.

Win felt his lawyer persona take over. Someone had to take charge and he couldn't help himself.

"Raylene, Toolie, why don't you take the ladies on back and finish whatever you were doing. Kenni and I are going over to the park." He grabbed two Cokes from the cooler before guiding her out the door and narrowly avoiding two kids on skateboards.

"Let's sit in the shade and you can tell me all about it," Win suggested. She remained uncharacteristically silent. He'd never seen Kenni without a comment on the tip of her tongue.

"Here," he said as he popped the top of the Coke can and handed it to her. "You need some sugar."

"YOU NEED SOME SUGAR?" Kenni barely suppressed a hysterical bout of giggles. Any Southern girl worth her mint julep knew that "sugar" meant a kiss. And yes, sirree, she surely could use some sugar.

He poked the Coke at her again. Oh, right. He meant real sugar. That's what she got for hooking up with a Yankee. Oh, wait—he said he was from Virginia, so he really couldn't be called a Yankee. Thank goodness!

A sip of caffeine and sugar was all it took for Kenni to pull herself together, at least well enough to respond to his questions.

"That was Teddy Errol Flynn. We went to elementary school together. He's a deputy now. Sheriff Dave knew we were friends, so he asked him to give me a call." Kenni sniffed before continuing.

"You know I got Bubba Gene some jobs mowing lawns, right?"

Win nodded.

"Anyway, Aunt Hallie Rule was one of those people. Anna Belle is her niece or something like that. She helped me talk Aunt Hallie into hiring Bubba. The woman's cranky, and rich, and lives in this big old house on the edge of town. She was lonely, and Bubba's such a nice guy. We all thought he'd be good for her. But, now she's dead, and her maid found Bubba Gene standing over her body with blood all over his hands." Kenni ended her explanation with a wail.

WELL, DAMN!

Not only did Win like Bubba Gene—who was obviously in big trouble—but this turn of events also meant the jig was up. Win was about to have his identity revealed.

There wasn't any way the gentle giant would kill someone, and Win wasn't about to allow an innocent friend to go down on a murder rap without a fight.

"Drink up, sweetheart, we'll go see the sheriff," he instructed.

Kenni gave him a glance filled with doubt but in the end she complied. More than likely it was because she didn't have a better idea.

Win followed her into the basement of the courthouse where the sheriff's office was located. Cop shops across the nation looked and smelled the same. Some enterprising entrepreneur had obviously cornered the market on metal desks, metal chairs and nondescript cubicle partitions. Then this unnamed person created a ubiquitous decorating scheme, cleverly known as bureaucratic BS. Add the sterile ambiance to the unmistakable aroma of stale coffee, musty paper and unwashed bodies, and Win was transported back to a world he knew.

"Hey, Miss Kenni, I'll bet you're here to see the sheriff. He said you'd be 'round purty quick."

"Yes, sir." Kenni gave the wiry deputy a gracious smile. Her Southern manners were alive and well, so she must be feeling better. Although Win suspected she'd use "yes, sir" and "yes, ma'am" even if she was in the throes of Ebola.

"He said to send you on back to his office. You know where it is."

"I sure do. Thanks, Harvey. I appreciate it."

On the way to their destination, Kenni stopped at almost every cubicle for a quick howdy. Why did the fact she was on a first-name basis with the entire police force disturb him? Could it be jealousy? No way, not Mr. D.C. Sophisticated. Jealousy wasn't his style.

Win was one of the best defense attorneys in the D.C. area and that was exactly the role he planned to resume. But how could he accomplish that objective without alienating Miss Kenni? Funny how he had started thinking in terms of Miss this, and Miss that.

It was that Southern thing again.

He was formulating a plan when the sheriff wandered in, a cup of coffee in one hand, a pile of folders in the other.

"Hey, sweetie. How ya doin?" he asked, before enveloping Kenni in a bear hug.

"Okay." she paused. "No, not really. Bubba Gene's my friend."

"I know. Why don't ya sit down and I'll tell you what I can."

When Kenni complied, he affectionately patted her on the head.

"He was found standing over Aunt Hallie's body with blood all over him. He's gonna need a hotshot lawyer, because—at least, at first glance—it doesn't look good."

"Uncle Dave, he doesn't have any money. He lives on social security, what he makes at my place, and his gardening jobs. Believe me, that's not much. And we both know he has the IQ of a third grader. He couldn't have killed her."

"I know, sweetie. Don't worry. The county has a public defender so he won't be without representation."

Kenni didn't bother to suppress her anguish. "Is Jimmy Arbuckle still the public defender?"

Dave nodded.

"That's freakin' fantastic. He cheated his way through high school. I'll bet dollars to doughnuts his law degree came out of a catalog."

"No, he really does have a law degree," Dave assured her.

"And I'll bet he was at the bottom of his class."

Dave didn't bother to dispute her claim.

"I want to help Bubba Gene but I don't have the money for a high-dollar Atlanta shark."

SHARK?

Despite her uncomplimentary assessment of his profession, Win knew he was going to help Kenni and Bubba Gene. He just needed some time to come up with a viable plan. One that would get Bubba Gene a "get out of jail free" card and still allow Win time to convince Kenni he wasn't a lying jerk.

Chapter Fourteen

It took a tag team effort from Win and the sheriff to convince Kenni to go home. In truth, it was Sheriff Dave's firm assertion that she wouldn't be any help, and that he wasn't about to let her see Bubba Gene in her current state of mind, that finally sent her home. Otherwise, Win suspected, they'd still be at the courthouse instead of sitting on her porch swing.

"What can I do?" She had asked the question at least three times. "I don't think there's any way I can come up with the money we'll need to defend him properly."

Win ran his fingers through her short spiky hair. "Let me ask you this. Why is it so important to you?"

She leaned forward, placing her elbows on her knees. "Years ago his mom was my Sunday school teacher. Then later she came into the salon at least once a week to get a shampoo and a set. She was such a sweetheart. She had Bubba Gene when she was quite a bit older. When she realized she was terminally ill, she asked me to keep an eye on him." Kenni gave Win a look he couldn't quite decipher. "He's functional to the extent he can work and live by himself but he can't handle money. So she put my name on his checking account. I guess in essence that means I'm his guardian."

Maybe that wasn't binding in the legal sense of the word, but it certainly placed a huge responsibility on Kenni's shoulders.

"Let's talk this out. First they'll appoint an attorney, and then there will be a bail bond hearing. The judge will either set bail or refuse it. The next step will be an arraignment. Let me assure you that even a guy at the bottom of his law class can handle a bail hearing and an arraignment. He'll tell Bubba Gene to plead not guilty." Win paused and then continued. "I feel sure that since a death is involved the case will be tried in Superior Court. That means we'll have time to come up with an acceptable attorney. Don't worry. It'll work out, I promise. You can take that to the bank."

WHO WAS THIS MAN? He looked like Win, he sounded like her favorite shampoo guy, but he was spouting terms like arraignment and Superior Court. The next thing she knew he'd be waxing rhapsodically about writs of habeas corpus.

Even in the upside-down world of Win's transformation, one word made a huge impression on Kenni—bail.

"What will I have to do to make bail?"

"More than likely it'll be cash or a bail bond. Do you have a couple hundred thousand lying around?" he asked. "In a murder case, that's probably what it will be. With a bail bond, you have to come up with ten percent, and the bail bondsman puts up the rest. No matter what happens, with a bail bond you don't get the ten percent back."

Good Lord! "I've read the Stephanie Plum books, and I've watched Dog on TV so I have a vague idea about bounty hunters, but I didn't know any of that stuff." She thought for a moment. "Do we even have bail bondsmen in this county?"

"I'm sure there's one. People get bonded out all the time. You just haven't noticed the office. Tomorrow morning before Bubba Gene's hearing we'll find it."

As much as she wanted to be independent and strong, just his use of the word *we* gave her a good feeling. Deep down she knew she could count on him.

Kenni kept telling herself that's why she let him pull her into his arms. He was dependable and responsible, and best of all, he made her feel safe and secure.

That wasn't the only thing that made him so attractive. He was much more than warm and fuzzy. Just looking at him elevated her temperature. He was hot and sizzlin', and off the Celsius scale with regard to sex appeal. He made her feel things that would make the ladies of the Methodist circle blush.

"Kiss me, right this minute," she demanded, slipping her hand to his nape.

"Yes, ma'am." He gave her a grin that was better than any aphrodisiac known to mankind. "I can certainly do that." And he did, right there on the porch swing in front of God and all her neighbors.

In the logical recesses of her mind Kenni realized their relationship was moving too fast. On the minus side—they'd only had one date, he was her employee, and—the biggest drawback of all—she didn't know a darned thing about him.

However, and this was a gigantic however, Kenni suspected she'd met her soul mate. Wouldn't that be a miracle? So to heck with convention and nosy neighbors and trying to control things that were uncontrollable. She could worry about all that later.

With that thought in mind, Kenni enjoyed the erotic play of his lips, tongue and very talented fingers.

Chapter Fifteen

The transition from the wonder of the night before to the reality of the criminal justice system was disquieting to Win even though he was a veteran of that world. He could imagine how it seemed to Kenni.

True to what he'd predicted, a high bail was set. The fact that the sheriff's entire family, and most of the patrons of Permanently Yours, had attended the arraignment obviously wasn't lost on the judge. And although it wasn't as much as Win had thought, a hundred thousand dollars wasn't chicken feed.

He followed Kenni and her family and friends out of the courthouse. The sheriff was a smart man and very aware of protocol, so he had to stay impartial. That didn't stop his wife from being front and center in the "Free Bubba Gene" movement.

For a few moments, Win didn't know where the entourage was heading, and then it hit him—Miss Melanie's Tea Room. The image of tiny bone china cups, miniscule scones and cucumber sandwiches with the crust cut off danced through his head. He'd skipped breakfast and he was ready for something that would stick to his ribs, but he resigned himself to minus zero calories and strolled in behind the ladies.

"So," Miss Anna Belle started the conversation. "Where are we going to come up with ten thousand dollars?"

That was a good question.

"I can toss in a thousand," Miss Eugenie said.

"Me, too." That offer came from Maizie and was matched by both Anna Belle and Liza.

"I can't go that high, but I can manage five hundred," Raylene contributed.

"Pencil me in for that much," Toolie said.

In amounts varying from ten dollars to two hundred, the women at the table offered cash.

"I have about three thousand in my savings," Kenni commented. "That still leaves us short."

"Don't worry about it. I'll make up the difference." That assurance came from Anna Belle's husband, Joe Nunn. He was the spitting image of the Kentucky Colonel and one of the nicest guys Win had ever met.

"Our problem now is to get him a decent lawyer," Joe continued. The women nodded in agreement.

They didn't realize Win had an ace up his sleeve—his partner and best friend, Colby Wharton—who, as luck would have it, had a license to practice law in Georgia.

That would remain his secret, at least for a little while, Win thought, as he slipped away in search of a phone. It was time to call off the bet and bring in the cavalry.

Win's biggest problem was how to pull this off without sending Kenni into orbit.

"HEY, COLBY. How are things going?"

"Pretty good, what's up?"

"Call me back. We need to talk." Win gave him the number of the telephone at the library. After a lengthy search he'd discovered it was the only working pay phone in town. The one at the convenience store was missing the receiver. What he wouldn't give for the cell phone he'd left back in Georgetown.

"Okay," Colby agreed without hesitation.

Win knew he wouldn't let him down. His friend was as reliable as a Swiss watch.

After Win explained the problem and outlined his plan, Colby agreed to return to Georgia to try the case.

"You're damn lucky I'm finishing up my current case. You've been down there less than three weeks and you're already knee-deep in a murder. I don't suppose you want to discuss our bet, huh?" Colby laughed at his own humor.

"Not right now. When can you get down here?"

"Give me a week or two. Things go pretty slow down there. I suspect we won't go to trial for a long time, and I have a couple of things to take care of here. You can prepare our strategy," Colby said. "You're better at that kind of thing than I am. But, I'll send Pete and Jillian down right away. They can get the investigation started."

"Okay. Have them bring my wallet. I need my credit cards."

Colby's raucous laughter reverberated through the phone.

Win made a rude remark that made his partner laugh even louder.

When Colby finally got himself under control, he delved into the details.

"Pete and Jillian will be down there day after tomorrow. They'll contact you."

"Make sure they do it on the QT."

"Sure thing. I can tell you're not in the mood to reveal your identity to the cute little blonde, correct?"

"I'm afraid so. At least, not this minute."

"Got it," Colby said, chuckling again. "You're about to get your platinum card back."

When he started humming, "You're in the money," Win pushed the disconnect button.

Chapter Sixteen

It had been two days since the bail bond hearing and the arraignment—two very long days. Bubba Gene had been bonded out and was living in Miss Anna Belle's guest house. He'd also resumed his janitorial duties at the salon.

Kenni had been so busy she hadn't had much time to worry about what was happening at work, or to find out what Win was doing. His sudden disappearance from the tearoom had been strange, but even more confusing was the fact he was making himself scarce. Every time she had a minute to talk, he made an excuse to leave. How could he avoid her after what they'd experienced on her porch swing? Was it a typical male "let's not talk about it," or was it something else?

The last customer had just left, and Kenni was in the process of locking up when she spotted Win walking toward the park. Not that she was spying on him, honestly she wasn't, but she couldn't force herself away from the window.

Win walked—amend that to sauntered, and Lord, could that man saunter—toward the gazebo where he met two people. It was obvious he knew them because he shook the man's hand and hugged the woman. Warning signs went up all over the place. Other than her friends, family and customers, Kenni didn't think he knew anyone in Magnolia Bluffs, and she didn't recognize that couple.

Should she ask Sheriff Dave to run a background check on her boyfriend, employee or whatever you wanted to call him? Oh, definitely yes. Assuming that Uncle Dave would handle the matter with finesse, Kenni picked up the phone.

"I need a favor."

WIN FELT GOOD following his meeting with Pete and Jillian. If it was possible to get to the bottom of the situation, they were the team to do it. They were the best investigators in the firm. And to make things even better, they'd brought him his platinum American Express and his debit card.

Hip, hip hooray! Win's days as a shampoo guy were numbered; so in the interest of preserving his fledgling relationship with Kenni, he had to do some mighty fast courting. A romantic date was the ticket. However, he couldn't magically come up with money, at least not until he explained the situation. Damn that bet!

Unfortunately, once a lie got legs, it took off and was almost impossible to run down. Kenni was worth whatever he had to do, up to and including some fancy knee walking. Win was contemplating the problem when Raylene joined him in the break room.

"Hey, good lookin'. What's with the big frown?"

"I'd like to take Kenni out on a romantic date. But with the Bubba Gene situation, I'm not sure exactly what I should do." Win finished his thought by holding out his hands.

"Oh, sugar. I get it. Let me assure you, she needs something to get her mind off her problems." Raylene assumed the Thinker pose. "Let me ponder this situation. We need candles and wine but you're on a beer budget. Not having wheels is a bit of a problem, too."

Win felt like a heel, but he let Raylene continue her brainstorming.

"A hamburger and a beer at the Dew Drop Inn won't work. So—" Raylene tapped her knuckles on the table. "I've got it."

Win almost jumped out of his skin when his coconspirator yelled, "Toolie, come back here, girl."

Great! Just what he needed—someone else in the loop.

"Keep your shirt on, I'll be there in a second," Toolie responded. These two women didn't use their inside voices.

"Where's the fire?" Toolie asked, smart-mouthed as usual.

"Win needs some dating advice."

"What?"

"You heard me. The dude doesn't have any cash but he wants to make a good impression on you-know-who." Raylene nodded in the direction of the front counter and ended her explanation with a wink and a grin.

Toolie retrieved a Dr Pepper from the refrigerator and popped the top. "Let me think." She rolled the can across her forehead as if she were participating in a mind-reading gig.

"What about this? The Kiwanis Fish Fry," Toolie suggested.

"You have *got* to be kidding me." Win couldn't suppress a snort. "Isn't that a bit…fishy?"

The women ignored his pun.

"I love them hush puppies," Bubba Gene said. He had joined them and was leaning on his broom, a big smile on his face. "Aunt Hallie used to make hush puppies, ya know that?"

Sooner rather than later, Win had to have a long talk with Bubba Gene. Somewhere in his memory, the man had the key to the crime; Win just had to ferret it out.

However, his concern of the moment was how to romance the boss. So it was back to discussing the Kiwanis Fish Fry.

"It'll work. I know it will," Raylene exclaimed.

Uh-oh. She was getting enthusiastic, and that might not be a good thing.

"It only costs $5.95 a person and it's all you can eat catfish and hush puppies. Best of all, it's held down at the river with lanterns and everything. I know where I can get you a canoe. What could be more romantic than a moonlight float on the water?"

The catfish cuisine part was dicey. A relaxing canoe trip had possibilities.

WHEN WIN SUGGESTED the fish fry, Kenni jumped at the chance to be with him again. It was a real date, with a meal he was going to pay for—even if it did cost a whoppin' big $5.95. So what if her uncle was doing a background check on him? And with everything she had on her plate, including being worried sick about Bubba Gene, she didn't have time for dating.

Who *was* she kidding?

Kenni's bedroom looked like a bargain basement dressing room after a clearance sale. Practically every piece of clothing she owned was on the floor or on the bed. She picked up a cotton sundress and tossed it toward the closet.

Jeans? Maybe. Halter top? T-shirt? No. She dug through her closet until she discovered a pair of daisy-yellow capris, a matching camisole and her new wedgie sandals. Bingo!

Kenni had just added a final spray of perfume when the doorbell rang. Wow—good-looking, sexy and punctual. What a combo!

And "wow" didn't come close to describing the guy standing at her door. What happened to the ever-present jeans and T-shirt?

"You look great." In fact, he was a sight to behold in a pair of Dockers and a pale blue polo.

"Thanks, and may I say that you're gorgeous."

Kenni couldn't put her finger on what was happening between them. For some reason they were behaving as if this was a blind date, and that was so far from the truth, it wasn't even funny.

She knew why she was acting weird. It was his clandestine meeting in the park. There had to be a logical reason. More than likely it was something innocent.

Right? And there was a wetland in the Mojave for sale. Of course that was her funky inner voice talking, and she almost always ignored the pest.

"Hey, big guy, I need a kiss," she demanded, grabbing the placket of his shirt and pulling him inside.

"I'm always ready to serve," he said, flashing a grin that could curl her toes. Then he laid a kiss on her that truly did curl her toes.

"I think we should get going while we still can."

"Uh-huh." Somehow she managed to express agreement without licking her lips. Would wonders never cease?

THE KIWANIS FISH FRY WAS the service club's annual fund-raiser. It was also one of the biggest social events of the summer. Volunteers were manning deep-fat fryers containing enough catfish and hush puppies to feed hundreds. Other members were dishing up side dishes and hosting the beer garden.

"This is fun," Win admitted, after he'd polished off a heaping plate of food.

"I like it." She paused, then asked the question she'd been pondering for a while. "Exactly where are you from?"

He waited a moment before answering. "Georgetown."

"I thought you said you were from Virginia."

"I was born in Alexandria." He didn't elaborate as he tossed their dinner debris in the trash and led her down to the river.

"What are we going to do here?" Kenni's curiosity was about to get the best of her.

"We're going for a romantic canoe ride. I need to talk to you."

"How about a kiss?"

"That, too."

Win helped Kenni into the boat, untied the mooring and then hopped in with her.

"I hope you know what you're doing." She hadn't been in a canoe in ages, so she was counting on his expertise.

"I think I do."

"Ooh-kay, that gives me a great deal of confidence." Kenni really wasn't as bothered as she sounded. She could swim, the river wasn't exactly fast-flowing and there was a ton of people on the shore.

Win paddled toward the other side of the river, allowing the canoe to drift under a canopy of low-hanging trees.

"We need to talk."

Under the best of circumstances, those were not words that evoked a great sense of optimism. Oh, well. If it was going to be awful, Kenni figured she could at least enjoy the moonlight.

"Kenni, I'm not—"

She failed to hear the rest of the sentence because his words were obliterated in a haze of pure terror. There was a snake hanging in the tree, right above her head.

A snake! A SNAKE!

Sheer horror blossomed into full-blown hysteria when she heard a loud plop and felt something wiggling next to her foot.

The folks in Atlanta probably heard her scream.

Before Win could figure out what was happening, Kenni had flipped the canoe and they were both treading water.

"Hang on to the boat," he ordered. "Can you swim?"

Instead of answering, she was off like a shot toward the opposite shore.

She wasn't exactly the most graceful swimmer he'd ever seen, but she was pretty darned fast.

Win had been on a swim team in high school so he was able to catch up with her. Her eyes were the size of dinner plates, her arms were flailing, and the only word she uttered was *snake* before she shot off like an Olympic contender.

Now he understood. It was time to put on the gas. Reptiles, particularly those of the aquatic variety, were not among his favorite critters.

Talk about an understatement!

IN THEIR FRANTIC RACE back to civilization, Win and Kenni made quite a bit of noise, so by the time they stepped onto dry land they had garnered an audience. Some kind soul provided a couple of blankets that smelled suspiciously like a wet dog.

Kenni had regained her sense of humor by the time they returned to her home.

"Look at that. Even Miss Priss won't have anything to do with me." She pointed at her calico cat who took one sniff, disdainfully stuck her nose in the air, and disappeared off the porch.

Kenni leaned over to smell Win's shirt. "Ooh, yeech. We'll put our clothes in the washer and then take a shower. How does that grab you?"

Apparently it grabbed him just fine—thank you very much—because he pulled her into his arms, nibbled all the way up her neck, and then proceeded to feast on her lips.

When they finally came up for a breath, Kenni's sense of propriety kicked in. She realized they had two options. Number one, stop what they were doing, or number two, go inside. Being the sensible, strong, independent woman that she was, she chose the second. Oh yeah!

"Inside," Kenni demanded, pointing toward the front door.

"Your wish is…"

Kenni didn't even allow him to finish his sentence. Without her knowledge or consent, her new motto had become more action, fewer words. She grabbed a handful of his blue polo and pulled him into her house, ready and more than willing to have her way with him. Not that he seemed the least bit averse to the whole idea.

The minute they cleared the portal, he backed her up against the door and slid the bolt to the locked position. And that was the start of Kenni's initiation into the true world of making love. Her entire relationship with Walter had been a sham on every level, particularly intimacy.

She knew she was a goner when he nestled his leg between

her thighs. He made quick work of the buttons down the front of her capri pants. They fell into a puddle by her feet, leaving only a thin scrap of material between the most sensitive of places and the rough denim of his denim-clad leg. Then all cogent thoughts went bye-bye when he pulled her stretchy camisole up and over her little lacy Victoria's Secret bra and proceeded to lick, suckle and generally drive her wild.

Never in Kenni's wildest dreams had she ever considered making love on the Aubusson carpet in her foyer.

But that was exactly what she did, and she savored every minute of it!

Chapter Seventeen

Win was still sporting a goofy grin when he woke up in Kenni's bedroom at the crack of dawn. The place was so girly it made his testosterone sit up and take notice.

He took a quick survey of his surroundings—the four-poster bed, acres of fluffy white material, and enough pillows to stock a mattress store. As far as decorating went, it was very pretty. Not his style, but very attractive.

His bed partner, on the other hand, was stunning. Not only was she gorgeous, she looked well-loved. A grin played across Win's face. He was responsible for all that mussed hair and her slightly puffy lips. Guilty as charged and proud of it!

"Hey, peaches," he whispered as he nuzzled her neck. Peaches fit her to a T. She had a peaches-and-cream complexion, and soft blond hair, and man, oh man, was she ever luscious.

"Hmm," she mumbled. He took that as an invitation to kiss her into the new morning.

Much, much later Win was still thinking about his incredible luck as he drifted back to sleep.

KENNI WAS in the middle of a scrumptious dream when an annoying bell kept intruding. In the fuzzy depths of sleep, she thought it was her alarm clock, and for some reason she couldn't turn it off. But finally, she realized it was the telephone.

What kind of apocalyptic news was out there ready to pounce? It was too early in the morning for ugly thoughts so she swatted them away.

When she rolled over, Kenni was more than a little aware of the man in her bed. He was adorable—almost childlike in his deep sleep. And no, she could attest to the fact he was anything but childlike.

Resisting the urge to run her fingers through the crinkly hair on his chest, she grabbed the cordless phone off her nightstand.

It was Uncle Dave. "Hey, sweetheart, I have some news about Win."

That woke her up. "What?" She grabbed her robe and was halfway down the stairs before Dave could continue.

"He's a criminal defense attorney in D.C."

"He's a what?" she squeaked. Under normal circumstances, she was the pragmatic, careful one. So how had he managed to get under her defenses? And what was he doing in Magnolia Bluffs?

"Do you remember Colby Wharton?"

Of course she did. His folks owned one of the biggest houses in town. "What's he got to do with this?"

"He's Win's law partner."

"I'm gonna kill him."

"Kill Colby?"

"Of course not, but Win Whittaker is a dead man."

"You want me to do it for you?"

The offer was certainly tempting, not that he was serious. "You're my favorite uncle. You know that, don't you?"

"Don't let your uncle Joe hear that," he said with a laugh.

"Yeah, but I still love you."

"Are you okay?"

"Absolutely. Tell Aunt Eugenie I'll call her later."

"Will do. Don't do anything I wouldn't do."

Kenni hit the disconnect button and stalked back up the stairs.

She was ready, willing and able to do some whoop-ass on the dude in her bed.

Win was still asleep. That was good, especially since he was at least a foot taller and eighty pounds heavier than she was. She doubted very seriously he'd take a pummeling lying down—no pun intended.

Kenni had to admit she was glad he was on the right side of the law. But, he'd led her to believe he was down on his luck. Homeless, her rear end. The guy was probably rich—weren't those attorney types all rolling in dough? And could she possibly have acted any more like a naive country girl?

Fueled by her ire, Kenni pounced on her victim, landing right in the middle of his delicious chest. She was oh so tempted to pop him in the nose. No, no, no. First and foremost she was a lady—somehow she had to dredge up a modicum of restraint.

"You're a scum-sucking liar." Kenni punctuated her declaration by tweaking his chest hair.

"Damn, that hurts!" He went from a deep sleep to being wide awake in two-point-two seconds.

"You said you needed a job, and to that I say kiss my lily-white rear end."

"Okay, I get it." He sat up, tossing her from her perch and scooting toward the headboard.

"You've obviously talked to someone," he said with a sigh.

"Yes, sir. I did."

He reached out to stroke her cheek, but retracted his hand when she hit him.

"Here's the truth and nothing but the truth. I promise." He crossed an X on his chest. "It started on a dark and lonely night."

Kenni responded with a nasty look.

"Honestly, it did. Here goes." Then he confessed everything from the inception of the wager to the present.

In a way, she was relieved. At least his picture wasn't on a post office wall. But he had a bet with his law partner! Talk about chutzpah. And what was going to happen to them? That is if there was a "them."

Win was a city boy. He couldn't possibly be happy in Magnolia Bluffs for any extended period of time. Instinctively, Kenni had known from the beginning that he'd turn her life upside down. She'd been right about that.

Would he stay or would he go? Was he rich or was he struggling financially? She didn't have an answer to any of those questions. Things were so topsy-turvy, she couldn't tell up from down.

The only silver lining was that he'd promised to help Bubba Gene—and the fact that she'd just had the most incredible night of her life.

Don't go there! She had to concentrate on Bubba Gene. Considering the circumstantial evidence against him, he was going to need all the help he could get. And that's where Win came in.

A little bit of God's meddling would be appreciated, too.

WIN FELT BETTER than he had in weeks. There was something to be said for confession. Now, if he could only decipher what Kenni was thinking. Normally, her face was like an open book. Too bad she'd decided to go for stoic this time.

None of that mattered because he was determined to turn their relationship into something lasting. Looking at the situation realistically, he knew he had a huge job ahead of him. That didn't matter because when Mr. Most Eligible Bachelor fell, he toppled like a ton of bricks.

"I know you have a lot to think about, so for now, I'll leave you alone." He stood, pulling her to her feet. "I have to go back to my office in D.C. for a couple of days, but I'm not giving up on us. I promise." He emphasized the vow with a long, hot, mind-blowing kiss, and leaned his forehead against hers.

"Sweetheart," he continued, "I'd better leave while I still can."
He gently swatted her on the butt. "But I can't go without my
pants."

"Oops. They're in the dryer."

Chapter Eighteen

Kenni's emotions were ping-ponging as she watched Win stroll down the sidewalk. She believed him when he said he wasn't walking out on her. On the contrary, as obstinate as he was, he was probably making plans to camp out in the middle of her life.

What to do, what to do? Kenni grabbed the phone and called in the troops.

"Hey, Liza, can you meet me for lunch? And bring Maizie with you."

"Need I ask if we're having a crisis?" her cousin asked with a giggle.

Oh, boy, news of their impromptu river dunking had probably spread like wildfire. "How about meeting me at the Mimosa Inn around one o'clock?"

"Yes, ma'am," Liza said, ruining her serious answer by breaking into laughter.

Kenni's next call was to Raylene to let her know she'd be late and that Win wouldn't be in at all. She made assurances she'd be in time to help with Traci Manning—aka Bridezilla—and her six attendants, scheduled for ten o'clock.

Just the thought of that appointment gave her a headache. "Do you have the champagne chilled?"

"Ab-so-lutely. Survival is the name of *this* game," Raylene responded.

Just as Kenni suspected, Traci alternately cried, giggled and issued orders. That was after consuming half a magnum of champagne. Short of stealing the bottle, Kenni couldn't keep the bubbly out of the girl's hands. From the looks of things, all the ladies had been tippling well before they'd shown up at Permanently Yours.

Ye gods!

Before the styling debacle was finished, the mother-in-law was blotto, the bridesmaids were about to mutiny, the bride had spent a good deal of the time in the restroom purging her meal, and Kenni had a raging headache. However, that wasn't the worst of it.

Kenni's biggest problem was that the bride had walked out of the salon with hair the color of an overcooked beet. She was a walking advertisement for salon malpractice. And it wasn't their fault, no way! Still, if they didn't get hauled into court, it would be a miracle.

"Remind me never to serve adult beverages to a bridal party ever again."

"Right on, boss. Keep in mind that you told her over and over and over what would happen if you put red/violet dye on her blond hair."

"I know. But I could've refused to do the color. I could've told her to go somewhere else," Kenni wailed, wringing her hands.

"She outweighed you by a good fifty pounds. I remember her from junior high," Raylene ruminated. "Even then she was as mean as a junkyard dog. That girl didn't hesitate to take on anyone who didn't toe the line. Personally, I don't think you had a choice."

Kenni slumped in her chair. "Intellectually I know all that. I just…" She shook her head in disgust. "What are people gonna think?"

"They're going to think she's a fruitcake," Toolie offered.

"When those two bridesmaids started yelling at each other about high-school boyfriends, I thought I'd pee my pants I was laughing so hard."

"I'm going to meet my cousins for lunch," Kenni said, grabbing her purse. "I've got to get out of here. Are you sure you don't need me for a couple of hours?"

"Nope, you go on and have some good girl talk. We heard about your dip in the river." In unison Raylene and Toolie broke into belly laughs.

"If a really big snake fell into your canoe, you'd be in the water before you could spit." Kenni barely resisted the urge to stick out her tongue.

"Probably," Toolie agreed. "I don't even like worms."

"So get going. We're fine," Raylene instructed, shooing her boss out the door.

THE MIMOSA INN WAS de rigueur with the Junior League crowd. It was the only place in town that served icy mimosas, wine spritzers, Earl Grey tea and tiny sandwiches. How girly-girl was that?

Under normal circumstances, Kenni didn't patronize the Inn. Their meals were barely big enough to keep a caterpillar alive. But these weren't normal times, and frankly, she wasn't up for the clatter and noise of the diner.

"Hey, sweetie." Liza gave her a hug before she sat down. "Maizie will be here in a few minutes. We're dying to hear what happened last night. Charlie was at the fish fry, and he said you kept muttering something about a snake. I hope you weren't talking about your date. I think he's cute."

So did Kenni, and that wasn't the problem. She was about to come up with an intelligent comment when Maizie arrived and the hugging ritual started all over.

Kenni had never been able to put anything over on her cousins, so she spilled her guts—everything from his profession, to the bet, to the…well, she didn't quite tell them everything. But she did say enough that they got the picture.

"Oh. My. God! I think I'm having a hot flash," Liza exclaimed before she chug-a-lugged half a glass of sweet tea.

"It's been forever since…"

"I know, honey." Maizie patted her sister's hand. After Liza's husband died she'd refused to get back into the dating scene.

"Now we can live vicariously through our favorite brat," Maizie said.

"I'm not a brat." Kenni's protestation was like fluff in the wind. "And you're happily married."

She didn't ask her cousins for advice about Win; she didn't have to. Just talking it out had cleared her mind. Now she was sure that if she didn't let their relationship—or whatever it was—run its course, she'd regret it forever. So fate had a green light.

"I hate to bring up an unpleasant subject while we're enjoying a mimosa, but what do you guys really think happened to Aunt Hallie?" Maizie asked. "And an even bigger question is what else can we do to help Bubba Gene? Bailing him out was just the first step. We still have to get him a good attorney, and I think we need to do some sleuthing of our own."

"Win didn't specifically say so, but I'm pretty sure his partner, Colby Wharton, is planning to act as Bubba Gene's attorney. That's one huge worry down. So what kind of sleuthing are we talking about?" Kenni asked. Although she was loath to admit it, she'd always harbored a desire to be like Maddie Hayes from *Moonlighting,* her favorite rerun.

Apparently Liza had read a couple of Nancy Drew novels herself. "Rumor has it that one of those big-box shopping centers is being proposed for the land between Aunt Hallie's place and old man Hardaway's swamp."

"Wasn't it Crumpy Hardaway's idiot grandson who tried to rob you?" Maizie asked. But before Kenni could respond, her cousin continued. "What was with the tea towel? Lord in heaven, couldn't the boy buy a ski mask?"

"Uncle Dave said he was going for the Ku Klux Klan look," Kenni said, shaking her head. "He couldn't be the murderer. He's in jail, although he does have a bunch of brothers and cousins, so I guess it's possible one of them had something to do with Aunt Hallie's death."

The cousins were contemplating the lack of Hardaway gray matter, when Liza spoke up. "Okay, back to the land deal, Charlie's roommate from Georgia Tech is a partner in one of the giant development companies in Atlanta. They're the folks who want to build the shopping center. He said that Walter is up to his kneecaps in the arrangement."

"Walter? My Walter?"

"Walter Harrington," Liza said in her best lawyer voice. "Do you want Charlie to get more information?"

Not only were Liza and Maizie on opposite ends of the spectrum looks-wise, their selection of profession couldn't have been any more different. Liza was a land-use attorney, who along with her pal, Charlie Taylor, had established a real estate development company. Maizie, on the other hand, owned a frou-frou store on Main Street appropriately named Miss Scarlett's Boudoir.

Kenni's mind was spinning a mile a minute. "I don't want to make life difficult for Walter. I'm positive he didn't have anything to do with Aunt Hallie's death. When we were married, I couldn't even get him to kill a spider." She shook her head. "Nope, he's not involved. So let's discuss the Hardaways. Do you think one of them could have killed Aunt Hallie to keep her from selling? Or conversely, one of them wanted her to sell, and she wouldn't."

The cousins nodded. "Who knows? They're certainly not very bright," Liza answered.

Kenni rubbed the bridge of her nose where a headache had taken up residence. "It sounds possible, but I don't know. It doesn't feel right. There was something really personal about the way she was killed."

"On the one hand, the Hardaways probably wouldn't want a shopping center cozied up next to the family home. Although if you looked at it in terms of money, they'd be rich enough so they'd never have to rob a beauty salon again. Or a convenience store or anything else."

"How about this for an idea?"

Kenni's ears perked up. Leave it to Liza to come up with a solution. She'd always been the family problem solver.

"Between the three of us, we know every gossip in town. We'll have some well-placed conversations and, you know—" she shrugged and grinned "—sort of lay out our suspicions. Then we sit back and see what pops up."

The woman was a genius. Although Win's professional investigators were undoubtedly excellent, they weren't good old boys, or girls, and the natives would never spill their guts to them.

"I think that's a great idea," Kenni said.

Maizie lifted her hand for a high five. "Me, too."

"Now, let's talk about the logistics," Liza said, always the planner. "We should also consider the possibility we're about to tweak the tail of a tiger."

"Oh, fiddle dee dee." Spoken as only the owner of Scarlett's Boudoir could. "No one in Magnolia Bluffs would dare lay a pinkie on us. Not with Uncle Dave in our corner."

"That's probably what Aunt Hallie thought," Liza reminded them.

Kenni was so busy thinking about her ex that she didn't comment. Could Walter be so desperate to get away from his mother that he'd do something illegal? No—not Walter. He didn't have the guts.

Chapter Nineteen

Two days had passed since Kenni's lunch with Maizie and Liza. Not surprisingly, they'd been able to implement their plan with ease. It helped that they had complete access to the town's leading salon and to the store that every woman in the county patronized. Kenni planted the seed with a couple of unrepentant gossips, and no telling how many people Maizie had cornered.

It had also been forty-eight hours since Kenni had heard from Win. Darn it—she knew he was in D.C. on business, but she missed him something fierce. Good employees were hard to come by and acceptable boyfriends were even more difficult to find.

Fortunately, she was saved by the bell; that would be the front-door chime announcing the arrival of the dingbat duo—Raylene and Toolie.

"Hey, boss lady, what have we got on the schedule for today?" Toolie asked, turning the appointment book around so she could read it.

"No. Please tell me I don't have to cut Mrs. Stackhouse's hair. It's not fair." Toolie hit her forehead with her palm.

Kenni couldn't resist a grin. "The customer is always right at Permanently Yours."

Raylene gave an irreverent snort. "Some of our patrons are two enchiladas short of a combo plate."

"I'll give you that one," Kenni conceded with a giggle.

Velda Stackhouse was truly one of a kind. Invariably, she came into the salon with dots painted all over her face—one on her forehead for the length of her bangs and matching dots on her chin and neck for the location of her layers. When all was said and done, the dots were supposed to connect.

Fruitcake city!

That bit of levity gave Kenni a much-needed reprieve from thinking about Win. As much as she trusted Raylene and Toolie, she hadn't confided her concerns about him or the murder. What could she say? *I'm pretty sure I'm falling in love with our shampoo guy, who by the way is a criminal defense attorney. And my cousins and I are trying to flush out a killer.* Even for Raylene and Toolie, that was too much information.

"Where's Win this morning?" Raylene asked.

"He's, uh…" Kenni's explanation was cut short when the subject of their conversation strolled in the back door. There he was, just as pretty as you please—faded jeans, scuffed boots, sexy grin and downright gorgeous green eyes.

"Ladies, are we having a staff meeting?" It was an ordinary question, but his velvety baritone made her think of hot fudge melting on homemade ice cream.

Yummy and decadent.

"Not without you, big guy," Toolie answered. "I was just griping about one of my clients."

Kenni was surprised that Toolie hadn't reverted to the junior-high flirtation of a combination hair flip and giggle. As it was, she managed only the giggle.

"Win, may I speak to you for a moment?" Raylene and Toolie hadn't moved an inch. "Privately."

"Sure." He gave her another one of *those* grins. "Ladies, I'll be back in a few minutes."

Her employees finally took the hint and wandered toward their stations.

To Win's credit, he waited until they were out of sight before he nibbled on Kenni's ear.

"What can I do for you?" he asked.

"Stop that," Kenni halfheartedly admonished him. "What are you doing here?"

"This is my place of employment, don't you remember?"

Kenni took his hand and pulled him out the front door. "Let's go to the park. We need to talk."

"Okey dokey," he agreed. "After you."

Kenni was in the mood for stomping; however, Win was more into strolling. So they strolled all the way to the gazebo. He sat down on the bench and stretched out his long legs.

The man was very comfortable in his own skin.

"I wasn't positive you'd come back to work. Not with the bet, and Aunt Hallie's murder, and everything." Kenni waved her hands to encompass the problems of the world, or at least her part of the planet.

"Sweetheart, I told you I wasn't going away. I simply had to go to D.C. to discuss the case with Colby." He picked up her hand and kissed the base of each finger.

Wowzer! He could do that again, and again, and again.

"You remember Colby, don't you?"

"Sure." How could she forget Colby Wharton? The guy had been the superstud of Magnolia Bluffs High School when Kenni was but a lowly freshman. That hadn't made them social equals—not by a long shot.

"Actually I don't know him, but I know of him." She laughed, thinking about all the girls who'd had crushes on him. "He was a major heartthrob."

"Really?" Win's grin spread over his entire face. "I'll have to rib him about that."

"Is he married?"

"Don't go there, little missy." He emphasized his command with one of those kisses that made Kenni think of romantic nights. Were public displays of affection legal in Magnolia Bluffs? Who knew, and even more importantly, who cared?

"Just for your edification, he's not married. The important thing is he's a member of the Georgia bar. So he can try Bubba Gene's case."

"That's great, I guess." Kenni had to wonder how successful their law firm was if they were able to drop everything and come to Georgia.

"It's better than great, because other than me he's the best."

Just the fact that someone competent was willing to help Bubba Gene gave Kenni a boost.

"Speaking of your employment, should I put up my Help Wanted sign?"

Win gave her a grin. "Hang loose for a week or two. I'm having fun with you guys. This is a long-delayed vacation."

Kenni gave him a friendly punch on the arm. "You have a weird sense of fun. Most people go to Maui for a vacation."

"But I wouldn't have met you if I'd gone to Maui."

Yep, that was the truth and nothing but the truth.

THE REMAINDER OF THE DAY was uneventful; that is, until the mail came. Then things went south.

If there was such a thing as a classic threatening note, the one Kenni received would qualify. It showed up in an innocuous white envelope and was mailed from the main post office. The text was cut out of the newspapers. And the sentiment was certainly chilling.

"This, this…piece of garbage says *Stop meddling, bitch*," Kenni exclaimed, barely suppressing an unladylike expletive. She hadn't been the recipient of a threatening note since the eighth grade, and that one had been from her primary rival for cheerleader.

"Put it on the counter, and don't touch it. Raylene, call the sheriff," Win instructed. "This isn't a joke."

Toolie was about to hyperventilate, and Raylene wasn't faring much better; however, she managed to grab the phone and make the call.

When Kenni took a deep breath and regained control of her emotions, she knew one thing for certain. Their well-placed questions had prompted someone to take action.

Win was *not* going to be happy when he discovered what they'd been up to. But on the bright side, if they found the note writer, they would unmask the killer.

And for sure it wasn't Bubba Gene. He couldn't spell bitch if his life depended on it.

Chapter Twenty

News of Kenni's note went through the family like Sherman through Atlanta. True to form, Maizie was the first to call.

"I want you and Win to come over for supper." The invitation felt more like a command than a friendly request. At first glance Maizie might appear to be a ditzy blonde. However, the term *steel magnolia* was custom-made for her.

"Liza will be here. We're due for a war council."

Maizie had obviously jumped to the same conclusion Kenni had. Someone in town was getting nervous. So what should they do about it? Pull the tiger's tail again?

"Do we really have to get the guys involved?"

"Yes." Maizie didn't elaborate or explain before she hung up. That girl was a natural-born steamroller.

"THERE'S SOMETHING I need to tell you before we get to Maizie's house." They were in Win's rental car, and Kenni had finally decided she had to tell him the whole story.

"Sounds like this might give me heartburn." Win's bone-melting smile tempered his comment.

"Well," Kenni started to sugarcoat her confession, but at the last minute went for full disclosure.

He slammed on the brakes and pulled to the curb. "You guys did what?"

The Harlequin Reader Service® — Here's how it works:

If offer card is missing write to: Harlequin Reader Service, 3010 Walden Ave., P.O. Box 1867, Buffalo NY 14240-1867

NO POSTAGE
NECESSARY
IF MAILED
IN THE
UNITED STATES

BUSINESS REPLY MAIL

FIRST-CLASS MAIL   PERMIT NO. 717-003   BUFFALO, NY

POSTAGE WILL BE PAID BY ADDRESSEE

HARLEQUIN READER SERVICE
3010 WALDEN AVE
PO BOX 1867
BUFFALO NY 14240-9952

Play the *Lucky Hearts* Game

and get...

2 FREE BOOKS and
2 FREE MYSTERY GIFTS...
YOURS to KEEP!

Yes! I have scratched off the silver card. Please send me my *2 FREE BOOKS* and *2 FREE mystery GIFTS*. I understand that I am under no obligation to purchase any books as explained on the back of this card.

Scratch Here!
then look below to see what your cards get you... 2 Free Books & 2 Free Mystery Gifts!

▲ DETACH AND MAIL CARD TODAY! ▲

© 2002 HARLEQUIN ENTERPRISES LTD.
® and ™ are trademarks owned and used by the trademark owner and/or its licensee.

354 HDL ELRR   154 HDL ELW4

FIRST NAME	LAST NAME

ADDRESS

APT.#	CITY

STATE/PROV.	ZIP/POSTAL CODE

(H-AR-08/07)

Twenty-one gets you
2 FREE BOOKS and
2 FREE MYSTERY GIFTS!

Twenty gets you
2 FREE BOOKS!

Nineteen gets you
1 FREE BOOK!

TRY AGAIN!

"We asked some leading questions. I think they got to the right person, prompting him or her to send that threatening note."

"Good God!"

"What can I say?" Kenni said somewhat sheepishly. "All's not quiet on the home front."

"This is not funny, Kenni," Win retorted, giving her a glare. After a few seconds, he put the car in gear and pulled into the traffic.

He was not happy, and she couldn't blame him. Interfering in a murder investigation wasn't the smartest stunt they'd ever pulled.

DINNER WAS a cordial affair, primarily due to the fact the conversation revolved around casual topics. It was Clay who finally got down to business.

"I talked to Dave. He's beyond pissed at you girls."

"Call me surprised," Kenni said. "Uncle Dave takes his oath to protect and serve seriously, especially when it comes to his family."

"So you talked to *my uncle?*" Maizie speared her husband with a look that could be accomplished only in a long-term marriage.

"Sure did."

"And you didn't discuss it with me first."

"Nope."

Brave man.

"Never mind that," Liza said. "We have to come up with a game plan, and Kenni's safety is primary. Does anyone have an idea?"

Win had a strategy in mind, but he wasn't sure Kenni would want it aired in front of her family. He wondered how she'd feel about a live-in bodyguard—him, of course. That discussion, however, required more privacy than they had at the moment.

His hand was on her thigh so he gave her a little squeeze. Initially it was an effort to comfort her. Then it quickly changed into something more sensual. It didn't take long for his heart to start racing and other body parts to come to full attention.

"Win and I have to talk." Kenni jumped up, pulling him with her. "We're going to the porch," she said to her hostess. "I'll be back to help you with the dishes."

She was halfway out the door before Win could catch up. He didn't think they could do what he *really* wanted to do on the front porch swing. *That* would land him in the county jail.

KENNI COULDN'T BELIEVE what she was about to suggest. Sure, she was nervous about the note. However, she recognized an opportunity when it dropped in her lap.

"I'd like for you to move into my house."

Win sat down on the porch swing with a thud. He hadn't quite made the mental segue from a sizzling seduction to something more practical when she made that suggestion.

"Really?"

Kenni joined him on the swing. "You can sleep on the couch if you want to."

"You've got to be kidding."

"Well…"

Kenni didn't get the chance to answer before he covered her mouth with his, giving her a long, lazy summertime kiss that went on forever.

Sorry to say, that was as hot as it was going to get on Maizie's front porch.

"Is that a yes?" she asked, when they finally took a break.

"Absolutely. And no couch."

"No couch."

"What are you planning to tell your cousins?"

"How about the truth?"

"Sounds like a plan to me," he agreed, following her back into the house. He certainly hoped Clay didn't pull out his twelve-gauge shotgun. That would be a real downer.

"HERE'S THE DEAL," Kenni said.

Maizie interrupted her cousin's explanation by handing her a plate heaped with dessert.

Hmmm, chocolate cream pie, her favorite. Explanations could wait, Kenni thought, her mouth watering at the mere idea of sticking a fork into all that yummy whipped cream.

Win obviously wasn't distracted by the chocolate pie. "I'm planning to move in with Kenni until we figure out what's going on," he announced.

At his statement, several forks stopped in midair. Clay, however, was the first to speak.

"Is that right?"

"Yes, and I don't want to hear any garbage about it," Kenni said around a mouthful of pie.

Clay waved his hands in surrender. "You won't hear a word from me. I can't guarantee what Anna Belle, or Eugenie or Sheriff Dave's gonna say."

Kenni shot Win an apologetic look. "I'll talk to them," she said, glancing at each of her relatives. "Your job is to make sure that news of my new roomie doesn't hit the grapevine."

"We can try," Liza agreed. "But you have the nosiest neighbors in town, so I wouldn't plan on keeping anything secret. Perhaps, that's not all bad. If our perp realizes you're living with someone he'll leave you alone."

"So now that your bodyguard is in place, what are we going to do about the threats?" Maizie asked.

"I think we should let Uncle Dave handle it," Kenni said. "The murderer is obviously someone we know. That's unfortunate because everyone in town was praying it would be a transient. I think it's important we keep this note a secret. That'll give the police a chance to do their job without interference. Perhaps they can get some fingerprints, or something, off it."

"Right on," Liza said, and everyone nodded in agreement.

"THAT WASN'T TOO BAD, at least not for an inquisition," Win commented as they drove toward his apartment above Permanently Yours to pack his belongings.

"I'm sorry you had to suffer through my relatives' questions."

"No problem, none at all." He shot her a sexy wink. "Especially not since I get to move in with you."

"Yeah." Kenni hated to admit she was having doubts about the wisdom of her idea. What *would* people think? Absolutely nothing got by her neighbors, and news of a guy moving into Chez McAllister would spread like wildfire. So should she worry about it now, or should she think about it later?

Later—definitely.

Chapter Twenty-One

Kenni felt like a voyeur as she helped him pack his clothes. He looked darned good in a pair of jeans; and he'd been even more handsome in the borrowed duds he wore to the wedding. She couldn't wait to see him in the expensive wool suit she was fondling. It felt like cashmere and it certainly wasn't an off-the-rack garment. So what was his financial situation? Not that it was any of her business. Yeah, right.

"Do you have everything?"

"Yep," he said, stowing the suits in a garment bag. "Now I do. Are you ready?"

That was an interesting question.

"Uh-huh." Kenni barely resisted the urge to bat her eyelashes. Coquettishness had never been her style. She was more of a "full guns blazing" kind of girl. "Let's go home."

"I'm positive I left my front porch light on. I always do," Kenni commented as they pulled into the driveway of her bungalow.

"It's probably burned out."

"I suppose I'm being skittish. Why don't you park here?" She indicated a spot near the front sidewalk. "After we unload, you can move your car to the garage."

Kenni had purchased her home shortly after the salon started showing a profit, and she loved it. Built in the early part of the twentieth century, it was quintessentially Southern with white clapboard siding, glossy black shutters, a wraparound porch and a cozy setting of white wicker furniture. Truman Capote would have felt right at home.

Although the gas lamp in the yard did little to illuminate the front door, something didn't feel right to Kenni.

Win turned off the engine and gave her an appraising look. "You're not comfortable with this, are you?"

Kenni realized he thought she was having second thoughts about his moving in. In response, she put her hand on his arm.

"It's not you, definitely not you. I just think there's something amiss, and I'm almost afraid to see what it is."

"Let me do it. Why don't you stay in the car?" He opened the driver's door but Kenni was faster.

"I'm coming with you." And she was right behind him. In the long run, whatever had happened in her home didn't really matter. Her only concern was her cat, Miss Priss. Everything else could be fixed or replaced.

"Oh, boy," Win muttered as he walked up the stairs.

"Here, kitty, kitty," Kenni cajoled, crawling under the bushes. Miss Priss was always on the front porch waiting to greet her. This time she was nowhere in sight.

Giving up her search, she followed Win up the steps, not quite sure she wanted to discover what he was muttering about.

Even in the gloom Kenni could see the bright red paint slashed across the front of her house.

"Bitch? He's not very original, is he?" Kenni reverted to humor to diffuse the situation.

"Sweetheart, don't worry." Win draped his arm around her shoulders. "I'm calling your uncle." He punched the numbers into his cell.

"I want to find my cat." Kenni walked down the steps and was on her way to the backyard by the time Win caught up with her.

"The guy might still be here. Wait till I get something out of the car," he instructed, sprinting back to the rental.

Nodding, Kenni sat on the step and watched as Win searched the vehicle.

Mission accomplished, he jogged back to the porch. "Let's find your kitty. I'm sure she's fine."

Kenni certainly hoped so. If the jerk had so much as touched Miss Priss, she'd hunt him down and neuter him.

The question was why was she thinking strictly in terms of a male? Kenni personally knew at least one female who was meaner than a pit viper. Namely Shelly Orwell, her best friend in junior high, the woman who had always been hot to canoodle Walter. And when everything went to hell, she went out of her way to rub it in.

To put it mildly, Shelly was nasty. And then there was Traci Manning. Sometimes people with bad hair went ballistic.

"Miss Priss has a bell, so if she moves you can hear her. I put it on because I thought the birds would be safer."

"Got it," Win said, poking his head around the corner of the detached garage.

"Listen." Kenni paused. "I think I hear her near the fence."

"Miss Priss. Here, kitty," she called.

Win stayed beside Kenni while she searched.

Several large camellias created a vegetative barrier to the alley. That's where she found Miss Priss—unhurt, but hissing mad.

"I've got her," Kenni said, cuddling the cat. "It looks like the cops have arrived." Flashing lights illuminated the neighborhood—so much for being subtle.

"Why don't you talk to them while I put her in the house? I don't want her to wander off again," Kenni said, already on her way to the back door.

"Sure," Win agreed, strolling down the drive as if he had the situation well under control.

"I'll be right there," Kenni called out, retrieving her keys and opening the back door. Life was spinning out of control, and she didn't know how to stop it.

Someone was threatening her! That was scary, but looking on the bright side, she'd scraped up the courage to ask the sexiest guy in town to move in with her.

In the annals of Kenni McAllister's life, it was a stellar moment.

THE GOOD NEWS WAS that Uncle Dave was taking the vandalism seriously. The bad news was that they'd need a lot more evidence to arrest anyone.

That was when Kenni decided that if she found the vandal before the cops did, she'd nail his hide to the nearest barn door. Rats on the legal system!

Uncle Dave's deputies finally left, the neighbors returned to their respective homes, and Kenni found herself cuddled on the couch with Win, a bowl of popcorn and Miss Priss.

"I'll paint the front of your house tomorrow." In typical male fashion, Win had commandeered the remote and was surfing the channels.

"I'm not all that concerned about the paint, although I'm sure the neighbors would like to get rid of the graffiti sooner rather than later. We have kids in the neighborhood." She popped a kernel in her mouth and chewed. "What do you think is happening?"

Win picked up a handful of popcorn. "I suspect you have an enemy, and your questions have stirred that person up. Can you think of someone who really dislikes you?"

"Everyone has an enemy. Traci Manning hates my guts, but I don't think she'd resort to graffiti because of a bad hair experience." Kenni thought for a moment but came up with the same answer. "Seriously, I don't have any real enemies. I'm a nice person."

"I agree." He then proceeded to show her how nice he thought she was. The ball game was soon forgotten.

Thank goodness she'd made a trip to Victoria's Secret. White Wal-Mart undies would not do the trick. Her lacy pink half bra and thong panties, however, were perfect. With that thought in mind, the daredevil in her took over as she pulled off her T-shirt and tossed it over the back of the couch.

Miss Priss hissed her disapproval and skittered off toward the kitchen. Win, on the other hand, was delighted.

"Does that mean what I think it means?"

"Oh, yes," she responded, emphasizing her intent by straddling his hips.

That wasn't nearly the extent of her newly found confidence…nor his appreciation.

Chapter Twenty-Two

"Did you hear what happened?" Liza exclaimed. She burst into Scarlett's Boudoir the moment Maizie opened the door. "I was over at the Coffee Klatch and Mrs. Stackhouse cornered me. The old bag was delighted to spread some news about our family."

"What did she tell you?"

"Kenni's house was vandalized last night."

Not only was Mrs. Stackhouse a pain-in-the-butt client of Permanently Yours, she was also one of Kenni's neighbors. Although normally her gossip was a bit suspect, this time she more than likely had her facts straight.

"Are you kidding?" Maizie plopped on her favorite antique fainting couch. "What kind of vandalism?"

"Mrs. Stackhouse said someone painted *bitch* in red paint all over the front of Kenni's house."

"That old biddy is such a snoop she checks out everyone who drives down the street. Did she see who did it?"

"No. She was at her sister's house in Macon yesterday." Liza frowned. "The one and only time she could have been helpful and she was out of town."

Liza sat down next to her sister. "I'm afraid we've stirred up a hornet's nest."

"Me, too. We need to get Kenni over here for a serious talk."

Maizie whipped the cell phone out of her blazer pocket. "I want to know what Uncle Dave said."

"Uh-huh."

"KENNI, PHONE FOR YOU," Toolie yelled. "It's Maizie."

Would that girl never learn proper telephone etiquette?

"Hey, Maizie. What's up?" It was a rhetorical question; she knew exactly why her cousin was calling.

"Get your cute little butt over here. Liza's here and we want to talk."

"What if I have a perm going? Would you want me to over-process it?"

"Goodness no. Do you? Have a perm in the works, that is."

"No, as a matter of fact my next client isn't due for an hour. I'll be there in a few minutes. I sure hope you guys have come up with something fantastic because I'm fresh out of ideas."

By the time Kenni walked the mere block to Scarlett's Boudoir, Maizie had turned over the Closed sign and Liza had broken out the good chocolate.

This had the earmarks of a major summit conference.

"Are you going to share?" Kenni was referring to the box of Godiva Liza had in her lap.

"Sure. Here." Her cousin handed her the chocolate. "After my talk with Mrs. Stackhouse I needed some endorphins."

"You talked to Mrs. Stackhouse?" Kenni couldn't suppress a groan.

"Yep. And the current rumor is that Win's down at the hardware store buying paint," Maizie contributed. "Did you by any chance tell him that to be able to cover red paint he had to put a primer on first?"

"What do I know about primer?"

"I'll call him." Maizie picked up her phone, but Kenni stopped her.

"He's a big boy, he can figure it out."

"Okay, guys, cut the discussion about paint. We have more important things to talk about." Liza always got down to the nitty-gritty. "First, of all, murder isn't common in these parts. However, in this situation we not only have a homicide, we also have someone—more than likely the murderer—threatening Kenni." She paused to munch on another chocolate. "So why aren't Maizie and I getting obnoxious notes?"

Good question; and one that didn't lend itself to an easy answer.

"Maybe it was someone I talked to," Kenni suggested.

"That would mean it was a woman. Or it could be a boyfriend, husband or significant other of one of your clients."

Kenni was pondering the possibility when Liza added a new wrinkle. "I deal with men every day. Not you guys. I should be getting the notes."

That was true. The number of men who patronized Scarlett's Boudoir could be counted on one hand; ditto for Kenni's clients. Other than a couple of guys who wanted a snazzy haircut, people of the male persuasion were not the mainstay of Permanently Yours.

"So let's assume for a moment that it's someone I contacted," Liza said with a sigh. "That could be just about anyone in the real estate development community. I told Charlie, but he knows what we're doing, and I also spoke to several lawyers, architects and engineers. Someone from that group would be a more likely suspect than anyone you guys talked to. Especially if we're right about the big box store center. So basically we're back to square one. Unless…" She paused. "Unless Walter is our guy. Then threatening Kenni would be more logical. From what I hear, he stands to make a lot of money if this deal goes through. Perhaps he thinks we're about to mess up his plans."

"God, I can't even think that way. We were *married!*" Kenni exclaimed. "I don't want to believe he could murder anyone."

Liza dropped the discussion of Walter and segued to the Hardaways. "Are we excluding Crumpy's family?" she asked. "He has more shirttail relatives than a coon dog has ticks. Someone could have talked to him."

"No way. We aren't excluding the Hardaways. In fact, they're my prime suspects," Maizie declared. "Crumpy's flat-out nasty. And the rest of his family is worse."

"Isn't that the truth," Kenni agreed.

"Why do you suppose his grandson tried to rob you?" Liza asked. "You don't keep a lot of cash at the salon."

That question had been bothering Kenni for a while, and she still didn't have an answer.

"I hadn't thought of that," Maizie said.

After a pause, Liza continued, "So exactly where are we in our investigation?"

"We know for sure that Bubba Gene didn't do it. He's not capable of hurting anyone."

"We can come up with all sorts of conjectures, but that doesn't get us any closer to a suspect. So I suggest we let Uncle Dave do his job." Liza had slipped into her "take charge" mode. "Our plan has successfully generated doubt about Bubba Gene's guilt and that was our primary goal. The unintended result seems to be that Kenni has to be very careful. Don't go anywhere alone," she instructed.

Although Kenni recognized the wisdom of the suggestion she couldn't resist a bit of sarcasm. "Yes, Mom."

Poor Win—he didn't know it, but he was about to become her constant companion.

Isn't that nice, Kenni thought with a smirk.

CONSIDERING THE EFFICIENCY of the Magnolia Bluffs grapevine, Win and Colby had decided to stage their investigation out of a neighboring town. Consequently, he met his investigators at a Denny's on the freeway.

"I hear we have a problem," Pete commented, digging into his Grand Slam breakfast.

Win had wisely passed on the cholesterol feast and was nursing a cup of coffee. "Yep, we do. I suppose you've also heard what caused this situation."

Jill grinned. "You have to give it to those ladies. They know how to pick a fight."

That would've been fine. In fact, Win would have applauded the effort if Kenni wasn't involved.

"Do you think you can capitalize on the fact that our boy's getting nervous?" he asked.

"There's nothing I like better than a jumpy bad guy," Jill said, sporting a huge grin. "I hear you've taken up painting."

Was nothing secret? "I certainly have."

"Did you remember to buy primer?" Jill asked.

"Is that something I need?"

"Positively." Her grin grew even wider. "I'll bet you hire someone to change your oil, don't you?"

"Okay, so I'm not handy. But I have other talents."

It was obviously the wrong thing to say because both of his investigators started laughing.

"Forget that." Win shook his head. "Let's get back to business." He'd briefly considered hiring a guard for both the salon and Kenni's house, but considering the *curious* neighbors, he'd quickly aborted that idea. Unless things heated up, he could handle the job.

"Colby will be down next week. We'll get together then. Same time, same place. In the meantime, if you find out anything, let me know immediately."

"Okay," Pete said.

"And pay special attention to the Hardaways," Win said.

"They won't be able to sneeze without us knowing it. And since we're gonna be watching so many people, Colby sent two additional investigators as backup."

"Who'd he send?"

"Larry and Jason."

"That's great. If you have any questions or anything to report, call my cell."

"Will do, boss," Jill said with a sly smile. "Be sure to buy some primer. If I hear of anything else you might need, I'll let you know."

Sheesh. Even his investigators were tuned into the grapevine. The next thing he knew, they'd be eating collard greens.

Chapter Twenty-Three

"Where is Win?" Toolie asked, popping the top on a cold Dr Pepper. She didn't wait for an answer before she continued. "Is he going to keep working or do we need to advertise?"

Those were good questions. Kenni didn't know his current location. However, she was positive he wouldn't be doing the shampoo job much longer. So yep, they'd better advertise.

"I think we should start looking for a new shampoo *girl*. And this time we're definitely hiring a girl."

"Darn it, the ladies are gonna be disappointed." That observation came from Raylene.

"And I'll miss having all those baked goodies," Toolie said.

That was true. Until Win came along, Kenni hadn't realized there were that many brownie recipes.

It was time to come clean about Win, his real life, the bet, and the fact he'd moved in with her. "I have something to tell you guys that's gonna blow your socks off." As she explained, she conveniently left out a few details, such as the sizzling hot nature of their relationship, and the fact that their cohabitation wasn't simply a matter of safety. That information would be shared on a strictly need-to-know basis.

"So are you going to take him to the garden party?" Leave it to Raylene to ask the hard question.

"With Bubba Gene and everything that's been going on, I haven't given it a thought."

"Bubba Gene would be very upset if you gave up a fancy party because of him. And, girlie, the shindig is this Saturday. I know for a fact you sent them a 'yes' RSVP, a long time ago."

Kenni vaguely remembered putting that in the mail. Auntie Anna Belle was the current Historical Society president, which meant that if Kenni wanted to remain a family member in good standing, she'd be going to the party.

"Should I take Win?" It was a rhetorical question. Of course she'd invite him.

"Yes," Raylene and Toolie yelled in unison.

"Even if this all started because of a bet?"

"Especially considering what he did to win the bet. From what you said, if he doesn't go to the party he loses. You don't want that to happen, do you?" Toolie asked.

"No, I don't." Her family would wholeheartedly approve of her date, especially Anna Belle and Eugenie. They had a soft spot when it came to Winston Andrew Whittaker IV.

Join the club. What red-blooded American girl wouldn't find him alluring? The man was charm personified, and at least this time they wouldn't have to raid the Haberdashery for something appropriate to wear.

"I suppose we can use it as his coming-out party. It will be our chance to introduce him to society."

"Right on," Raylene agreed. "How about that, Win's gonna be Magnolia Bluffs' newest debutante."

KENNI HAD JUST DEPOSITED her client under the dryer when she heard an argument up front. Not again! When she spied the source of the altercation, her stomach did a somersault. It was Traci Manning, aka Bridezilla, and her hair was even worse than before. Fortunately she hadn't been back since the wedding-day hair fiasco, but that woman was a salon owner's worst nightmare.

"Hi, Traci." Kenni decided to go for being friendly.

"Don't you *hi, Traci* me, you bitch," she yelled. Spittle flew all over the counter. "You've ruined my life. My husband can barely look at me without laughing. I couldn't face another trip to a beauty salon, so I decided to fix it, myself," she wailed as she lifted a strand of ruined hair.

Kenni was almost knocked over by the fumes. Big uh-oh. Traci was not only mad, she was plastered. Kenni hoped she wouldn't get violent, but with an irate customer nothing was a certainty.

"Traci, why don't you come on back with me? We'll see what we can do to fix it," Kenni said, steering the woman toward the rear of the salon. As they passed Raylene, she mimed a phone call, and mouthed "if necessary."

Raylene nodded, surreptitiously holding up her cell.

Kenni pushed her unwilling client into the chair and somehow managed to get a cape around her neck. Lord in heaven, what had happened? If she got this stuff looking like real hair again, it would be a miracle.

"Did you try to color it yourself?"

Traci hiccupped. "Yeah, that purple stuff sucked."

"Raylene, would you come here a minute? I need another opinion."

Raylene strolled over and studied Traci's head from every angle. Then she called Toolie.

Toolie's advice was succinct. "Cut it all off. There's not much you can do for it now."

Traci's wail—one that incidentally could have been heard in the next county—left no doubt as to how she felt about the suggestion.

It took almost an hour of cutting and conditioning before Traci was presentable. The style wasn't great—to say the least— but it was acceptable, and that was a huge improvement.

"Do you think she appreciates what we did?" Toolie asked as they watched Traci slam the door.

"Nope. We're convenient scapegoats for everything that's going wrong in her life," Kenni said. "Why don't you guys go on home? I'll clean up. I think Win might be coming by in a little bit."

"I'm out of here," Raylene said, heading for the front door. Toolie was a half step behind her.

WIN PARKED in the small gravel lot behind Permanently Yours. His plan was to take Kenni out for a romantic dinner, complete with candles, wine, flowers and cuisine that didn't come out of a sack. The courting was about to begin.

It was almost six o'clock, so all the clients would be gone. At this time of the afternoon Kenni was usually in her office doing paperwork. Win fingered the velvet petals of the two dozen pink roses he'd picked up at the florist.

Although he wasn't sure how things would eventually work out, he knew with absolute certainty that he was in love. If it meant doing a complete one-eighty on his professional life, so be it. Defending the dregs of D.C. society had lost its appeal, and money wasn't an issue.

A strange noise jerked his thoughts back to the present. What was that? Another crackling sound came from inside the shop, and Win was out of the car in a flash.

The door was always unlocked during business hours and more than likely Kenni hadn't secured the alarm, so Win didn't bother digging in his pocket for a key. He jerked the door open and caught a whiff of smoke.

Where was the fire?

He frantically scanned the storeroom to determine the origin of the flames and almost immediately spotted a wisp coming from the bathroom. Where was that darned fire extinguisher?

"Kenni, Kenni," he screamed. "Call 911. We have a fire." He

hoped she could hear him. Sometimes she did computer work with her headphones on and the music cranked up. When she was tuned in, elephants could stomp through the shop and she wouldn't hear them.

Dredging up all the information he'd ever learned during Fire Prevention Week, Win gingerly touched the door. Releasing a firestorm would not be a good thing.

"Fire! Where?" Kenni squealed, making an appearance in the connecting doorway.

"The bathroom. Call 911," Win instructed without turning.

The door was fairly cool to the touch. That indicated the fire hadn't taken control; however, he didn't have the luxury of waiting for the fire trucks.

Win relied on good common sense as he carefully opened the entrance, ready to slam it and get out of the building if necessary.

Whew! The flames were confined to a pile of paper in the corner. And unless mice were now playing with matches, an arsonist had left his calling card. Fortunately the firebug wasn't a professional, but fire was fire. And any conflagration had the potential to kill.

Win put those dire thoughts on hold. First things first, extinguish the flame, then find the son of a gun who started it. Lord pity the guy if Win got his hands on him.

By the time the authorities arrived, he had smothered the fire. However, the smoldering garbage was causing a significant amount of residual smoke.

KENNI WAS TRYING her best not to kick, scream or generally pitch a hissy. Threatening notes were bad enough, but this time some idiot had attacked her salon. She was *not* amused; in fact, she was close to being homicidal.

Permanently Yours was her baby! Nobody messed with Kenni McAllister and got away with it.

Chapter Twenty-Four

Although the front of the salon wasn't affected, smoke damage had made business as usual impossible.

Kenni grumbled and groused, and eventually realized all the griping in the world wouldn't remedy a thing. So she calmed down, called the repair people, locked the door and decided to worry about the details later. Insurance would cover the damage, and all things considered, she could use a couple of days off.

"Let's go home and get cleaned up. I smell like a bonfire." Win pulled the hem of his shirt up to his nose.

"Uh-huh," Kenni agreed. Wow. That man had world-class abs. But how could she be thinking about sex when an arsonist had wreaked havoc on her business? It had to be a delayed reaction to stress, or one of those "let's go party 'cause I almost got hit by a bus" kind of things.

"Before we do anything else I have to call Raylene and Toolie to let them know what happened. And if I don't tell my family about the fire, I'll be disowned," she said with a half grin. "Then I need to reschedule the next couple of days' appointments."

"I'll help." He pulled his cell phone out of his pocket and steered her toward his car.

Darn it—she'd weathered the crisis of the fire and graciously made it through the fire marshall's questions, but the bouquet of roses did her in. One look at the beautiful pink flowers and the dam of tears burst.

Some guys ran at the first sight of a female crying. Others reverted to sarcasm. Win, however, proved to be a trouper.

"Don't worry. Things will work out." He pulled her into his arms and let her use his shirt as a towel.

With him, there wasn't any of that awkward back-patting. Walter had been especially uncomfortable with emotional displays, but he'd been embarrassed about almost everything she did.

Kenni wiped her nose on her sleeve and gave a final sigh. Miss Alicia, the etiquette guru, would have a fit, but hey, Kenni had more important things on her mind.

"A shower sounds like heaven." She winked at her best guy. "Or maybe a leisurely soak in the tub. Would you like to share?"

"Absolutely!" Win hit the gas pedal like a rookie NASCAR driver.

KENNI WAS EXPECTING a nice long bath for two, a romantic dinner and some good lovin'. But somewhere between Point A and Point B, Win had decided on another agenda and being a typical male, he hadn't bothered to share. He was in and out of the shower so fast he barely got the tiles wet, and off he went with a phone stuck to his ear.

Well, at least she was clean and her hair didn't smell like the inside of a barbecue, Kenni thought, as she marched into the kitchen. Not much solace when she'd had an erotic agenda in mind.

The refrigerator door barely withstood the assault as she jerked the door open. It was wine time. She popped out the cork and poured a liberal dollop into a plastic Big Gulp cup.

Kenni didn't get miffed often, but when she did, it was a sight to behold. The cousins claimed she was downright scary. They called it her Brunhilda mood. What did they know? She took another slurp and slammed the cabinet door.

He was the last guy on the planet she'd ask to the garden party. No way, no how!

WIN PUMPED A FIST in the air. Going away for the weekend was a stroke of genius, and he hadn't wasted a minute in implementing his great idea. In a matter of minutes he'd scored a reservation at an exclusive resort in the Georgia foothills. Kenni was due for some pampering, and he was looking forward to a weekend of indulging her.

Win was flushed with success. He couldn't wait to give her the good news and receive a kiss as his reward. "Hey, peaches—" He never got the chance to complete his sentence.

"Don't peaches me!"

Uh-oh. He was in a mess of trouble and he didn't have a clue what he'd done. It was a worst-case scenario for a guy.

"I, uh—"

Kenni interrupted him, grabbing her cordless phone. "I'm calling for pizza."

She didn't bother to ask whether he liked pepperoni or pineapple. That wasn't a good sign, and her glittery green eyes were definitely not an encouraging omen. He'd heard about Brunhilda from the cousins, but up to that point he hadn't actually met her. And he wasn't sure he wanted to make her acquaintance now.

Despite all odds, and being the brave guy he was, Win marched into the fray. On the silver screen cowards never got the girl. And, by gosh, he planned to snag this heroine. A sneak attack was in order—complete with kissing, and nuzzling, and whatever came next.

"I'm—"

He didn't give her the chance to complete her thought.

"Shh," he demanded, slanting his lips over hers, then he moved down her neck toward his ultimate destination.

When they finally came up for air he went on the offensive. "I'm sorry."

When in doubt, an apology was always in order. It was a lesson he'd learned early in his dating experience, and if past history held, it had about a fifty-fifty success rate.

"Hmm," she murmured, pulling him down for another kiss.

That was good. Actually, it was fantastic. Forgiveness *was* in his future, and hopefully there'd be some R-rated adventures, too.

A COUPLE OF HOURS LATER, they took a water-saving shower for two. "I have a great idea," he ventured, running his fingers through her wet strands of hair.

"Uh-huh?"

"I've made reservations for us to spend a couple of days at the Willow Tree Resort."

"You've done what?" She backed up a step.

Win garnered all his powers of persuasion. "Since you can't open the salon and you've made arrangements for the cleanup and repair, I thought you'd like to get away for a little while. How does a massage, a canoe ride in the moonlight, and some quality time with me sound?" Win had resorted to cajoling and he was more than willing to beg if necessary.

"It sounds good. Where's the Willow Tree?"

"It's in the foothills about an hour and a half from here."

"It sounds terribly tempting."

"Yes, ma'am." He punctuated his agreement with a long, slow kiss.

"And I'm sure Liza will be glad to keep Miss Priss," she muttered. "So kiss me again."

How could Win resist? He was, after all, a red-blooded American male in a very small shower enclosure with an incredibly delectable female. He loved her and he planned to spend the rest of his life with her.

Chapter Twenty-Five

The next day, they got a late start, so it was early afternoon before Kenni and Win reached the Willow Tree.

"I didn't know a place like this existed," she said, surveying the grounds of the resort. It was a delightful surprise. The groupings of cottages were connected by lush English-style gardens and a tree-lined walkway.

The brochure she'd picked up at the registration desk indicated the manor house was originally part of one of Georgia's earliest plantations. However, time, economic spirals and war had taken its toll until eventually the land was left to go fallow. Enter an insightful entrepreneur who bought the property for a song and resurrected Willow Tree's former glory.

"It is nice, isn't it," Win agreed, surrendering his car keys to the valet. "My incredibly efficient assistant found it on the Internet and booked it for us."

"Thank her or him for being so resourceful," Kenni said with a smile. She was savoring the array of flowers and the addictively sweet scent of honeysuckle. And while she didn't verbalize it, Kenni thanked her lucky stars for having a thoughtful guy like Win in her life. The survivor of a failed marriage, she knew all too well that not many men were cut from that cloth.

Win glanced at the packet the desk clerk had handed him. "It looks like we're staying in the Wisteria Cottage. Sounds nice, doesn't it?"

"Mm-hmm." Kenni was so engrossed in checking out the surroundings, she almost didn't answer. The place was romance at its best, and they hadn't scratched the surface of possibilities.

Kenni had needed a vacation for a long time, but for a variety of reasons she hadn't taken the time. Perhaps she'd simply been waiting for Win.

Wisteria Cottage was the essence of daydreams. With its red brick façade and trellis of lush purple wisteria, Snow White would have loved it.

So was Win her prince? Only time would tell.

"Oh, my," Kenni murmured, savoring the interior of the cottage. "It's simply beautiful." Antiques, a wood-burning fireplace, tall ceilings and fresh flowers created a cozy, but elegant, ambiance.

Win wandered off toward the bedroom. The man was as transparent as a piece of Saran Wrap.

Kenni followed him. Okay, she'd admit it. She'd had the same idea.

The living room was lovely, but the bedroom exceeded all expectations. The antique sleigh bed was fit for a princess.

"What do you think about checking out the accommodations?" Win asked, putting his arms around her and nudging her toward the edge of the mattress.

He didn't have to ask twice. Kenni fell into the middle of a pile of pillows.

"The bellboy will be here in a few minutes," she reminded him, as he removed his belt and pulled down the zipper of his trousers.

"Oops, I forgot." Win frowned as he restored his clothing and strolled toward the front of the cottage, not a minute too soon.

The situation with the suitcases settled, they could get down to the fun stuff. Could they ever!

KENNI RAN HER FINGERS through his crisp chest hair, massaging his rock-hard abs in the process. That felt so good she could do it all night, and she was absolutely positive he wouldn't object.

"If you keep that up, we'll miss dinner." He captured her hand and kissed her palm.

"Dinner, bed, dinner, kissing. Do I really have to make a choice?" At that point Kenni's stomach expressed an opinion.

"That settles it. We're heading to the dining room. When we get back, I suggest we check out the claw-footed tub."

"Sounds like a plan." Kenni's agreement was punctuated by another tummy rumble.

"ARE YOU ENJOYING YOURSELF?" Win asked toward the end of a scrumptious meal.

"Of course." Kenni couldn't keep the smile off her face. She was having a romantic adventure with the man of her dreams—forget the nasty stuff back home. There was, however, the tiny problem that they'd never discussed significant things like finances, and even more important, their relationship. As far as she was concerned, the love thing was easy. She was head over heels crazy about him.

The finances were another matter entirely. The menu prices at this place were enough to make your eyes water, and God only knew what he was paying for the room. Could he really afford it? He was an attorney, but that didn't necessarily mean he was flush with money. Some of the lawyers she knew were barely making ends meet.

So Kenni did what she thought was the sensible thing and suggested they go Dutch treat. That was met with a resounding *no way.* Stubborn man! When he mentioned a day at the spa, Kenni countered with the option of a hike. She pointed out that there were also some free adventures they didn't have to leave the cottage to enjoy.

"Let's skip dessert and go back to the room. I'm feeling like a bath," she said with a grin.

Before she could blink an eye, Win hailed the waiter and paid their check.

Lord, you had to love an enthusiastic man—especially one with slow hands and a passionate heart.

Chapter Twenty-Six

Win had muscles on muscles, Kenni thought, as she watched him row. Sure, she could take a turn with the paddles, but why spoil the view? As a surprise he'd ordered a gourmet basket for them to enjoy at the picnic area across the lake.

"Are you planning to help?" he asked, with the quirk of a smile.

"And ruin the macho thing?"

"You're right." He gave her a wink and a grin. "Sit back and relax."

He didn't have to ask her twice. The past couple of weeks had been mentally exhausting. Plus, they hadn't had much sleep last night, and the glide of the boat was so peaceful. With the warm sun on her face and the country sounds in the background, Kenni drifted off to slumberland.

Suddenly her peaceful interlude was interrupted by an explosive noise that ripped through the quiet. Win shouted an expletive as the canoe tipped over.

Not another snake! Kenni slowly drifted toward the bottom of the pond. Her brain and muscles weren't on the same page.

Fortunately, Win had his act together and pulled her to the surface. "Someone's shooting at us. Swim underwater as far as you can. Don't come up until you absolutely have to, and go in that direction." He pointed toward the dock behind their cottage.

He didn't have to ask her twice. This was far worse than a threatening note, or even a snake.

"You're coming, aren't you?" she squealed.

"Right behind you."

Another shot rang out as the pair ducked underwater.

This was getting damned old. She was not *ever* getting in a canoe again!

ONE OF THE ground maintenance people witnessed the incident and reported it to his superiors. Their 911 call prompted an emergency response, and within thirty minutes the cottage was swarming with cops and resort management. Less than an hour later, investigators from the Georgia Bureau of Investigation arrived.

Kenni and Win had changed clothes and were sitting together on the couch. He was holding her hand making her feel somewhat better, not top of the morning, but better.

"What do you bet a team of lawyers is on its way from Atlanta?" Win commented as he squeezed her fingers.

That was a no-brainer. Of course the attorneys were making a mad dash to the Willow Tree. Having guests shot at while on resort property was a huge liability issue. But a lawsuit was the last thing on Kenni's mind. All she wanted to do was go home and slam the door on the rest of the world.

"The minute we're through giving the investigator our statements, we're leaving," Win informed the manager, interrupting his litany of innocent possibilities ranging from errant hunters to firecrackers.

The explanations were a crock. Someone had advanced from fear tactics to attempted murder, and that scared Kenni right down to the tips of her pink-painted toenails.

"The minute we hit the Magnolia Bluffs city limits, I'm heading over to talk to Dave. This has gone far enough," Win declared, not taking his eyes off her.

Amen to that. "I'll call him and tell him we're on our way. Knowing him, by the time we get to Magnolia Bluffs, he'll be sitting in front of my house with the lights flashing."

THAT WAS EXACTLY what Win was counting on. He'd almost swallowed his tongue when he'd realized the noise was gunfire, and it was aimed at them.

Hell—that would have rattled anyone.

The ride home was ominously silent. Kenni had shut down— no tears, no ranting, nothing. It was so un-Kenni-ish that it threw Win for a loop. How did he handle the silent waif huddled in the passenger seat?

That became the least of his problems when her cell phone rang.

"It says pay phone on the caller ID," she muttered, the color leaching from her face.

Win moved to the side of the road and cut the engine. "Answer and hold it up so I can hear, too."

The voice was electronically altered, so it was impossible to discern whether it was male or female. The message, though, was loud and clear.

"I told you to stop meddling and you just kept at it. The shot was a warning—the next time I won't miss."

Kenni snapped the phone closed. "That makes me absolutely furious!"

Win was almost glad to see her get agitated; it was much better than the melancholy.

"I want you to stay away from me," she declared, turning her face toward the window.

"What?"

"Stay. Away. From. Me. Is that clear enough?"

Win resisted a chuckle. This tiny Peter Pan wanted to protect him, but being the smart guy he was he didn't crack a grin.

"Let's not discuss that. At least, not until we talk to Dave."

She shot him a grim look. Stubborn was her middle name. Well, that was too bad. He *wasn't* intimidated.

Chapter Twenty-Seven

"Tell me exactly what happened." Sheriff Dave was sitting on her couch with a notebook in one hand and a cup of coffee in the other. In some ways it felt like an ordinary visit. However, when Uncle Dave visited, he usually ditched the gun and uniform. This time he was in full regalia. Not only that, he had on his cop face.

Win glanced in her direction. "Kenni and I went up north for a little getaway. We hadn't been at the resort more than a day when someone took a potshot at us. We were out in a canoe when it happened."

"Are you sure it wasn't a hunter with bad aim?"

"Positive. The GBI didn't think so, either."

"Can't argue with the big boys," Dave admitted. "Did you get a look at the guy?"

"No. I was busy rowing, and Kenni was napping. I can give you the name of the GBI agent in charge of the investigation. The folks at the resort are very nervous, so I suspect a thorough search of the area was done."

"You guys don't have good luck with boats, do you?" Dave asked with a chuckle. "I'll wager those hotel folks are about to hack up a fur ball worrying about litigation."

"And I'm not about to disabuse them of the idea. At least, not

until we get some answers. But that's not the worst of it. Kenni
got a threatening phone call on our way home."

"What did the caller say?" Sheriff Dave demanded. At that
point he was all business.

Win relayed the conversation verbatim.

"Well, damn," Dave exclaimed, and then he paused for a
moment before continuing. "I have an idea, but I'll need Kenni's
help to pull it off."

"I'm willing to do anything you want." That was her first contribution to the conversation.

"Okay, here it is. This garbage started when you girls tapped
the rumor mill. I think you should talk to Laverne Hightower and
see what she knows." Dave chuckled. "Right now I'm not her
favorite person, or I'd do it."

Kenni chewed on her bottom lip, then smiled. "That's a great
idea. And you're absolutely correct. She *wouldn't* let you in the
house. I heard she got her tail feathers all fluffed up when you
had her car towed."

"What else could I do? She left it in a loading zone for three
days."

Win was at a loss. Who were they talking about? Then he remembered the octogenarian from the salon. Sometimes it felt as
if the people in Magnolia Bluffs spoke a foreign language.

Kenni took pity on him. "Miss Laverne is the lady who identified Crumpy's grandson after our robbery. She knows everything that happens in this town. In fact, she has dirt on almost
everyone in the county. And no one can figure out how she does
it, because other than coming to the salon and going to church,
she's a hermit. I do her hair, but she still scares me."

"Don't worry, I'll go with you," Win said. "I don't think we
have much choice."

Kenni flipped open her cell phone, and while she was talking
to Miss Hightower, Win broached another subject.

"Dave, I think you should have another long talk with Bubba Gene," he suggested. "Maybe if you ask some different questions he might dredge up something new."

"It's worth a shot," Dave agreed. "I've talked to him myself and my detectives have questioned him, but perhaps we weren't approaching him the right way."

"OKAY, GUYS, she's expecting us in an hour, and she's really excited about Win coming."

"I can't wait," Win said with a wry smile.

"You need to learn to control that sarcasm," Kenni admonished him with a giggle. The poor guy looked about as eager as a kid trudging to the principal's office.

KENNI OPENED the creaky gate of the picket fence and walked up a path overgrown with vines and trailing roses. "I don't know if you remember, but Miss Laverne is somewhat eccentric."

"That's nothing unusual. Just about everyone in this town is eccentric."

She ignored his comment as she tapped on the front door of the gingerbread Victorian. Win picked at a strip of peeling paint on the doorjamb.

"Stop that," Kenni demanded, tapping his hand.

"Hi there, Miss Laverne. You remember Win from the salon. He washed your hair."

"Of course I remember him. I might be old as the hills, but I'm not addled. Come on in. I've made some fresh lemonade." Laverne opened the screen door and ushered her visitors inside. In a move worthy of cotillion queen, she grabbed Win's arm and batted her eyelashes.

Kenni couldn't resist an eye roll as she followed Win and Miss Laverne into the house. She felt like a third wheel.

There were just some things you didn't rush, and Southern

hospitality was at the top of the list. So, they spent an hour snacking on lemonade and sugar cookies. Finally Kenni worked up the nerve to ask the big question.

"There's something really important we need to find out."

"What is it?"

"It's about Aunt Hallie's murder."

"Poor woman, things like that shouldn't happen around here. Whoever did it needs to be strung up. Don't know why they don't do public hangings anymore. That would put a halt to crime."

"Yes, ma'am," Kenni murmured, leaning forward to ensure she had the older woman's attention. "We're trying to find out if anyone saw or heard anything at Aunt Hallie's that day, and for whatever reason they haven't come forward."

Laverne rested her chin on her hand. "Let me see, hmm. Wonder what Stanley Cook knows? Not that the old coot remembers his own name most of the time," she muttered to herself. "He's Aunt Hallie's back-alley neighbor."

Kenni glanced at Win. She could tell he was trying to stifle a grin. Who could blame him? This wasn't exactly a Sherlock Holmes moment.

"By gosh, I think he *is* the guy we need to talk to. Let me give him a buzz just to make sure I'm right." Laverne searched through the pile of papers and magazines on the coffee table in an attempt to find her phone.

"Hey there, Stanley. Welcome home. How's Miss Maude doing?" There was a long silence before she spoke again. "You tell that sweet wife of yours to keep her feet elevated and get lots of sleep. She'll be fit as a fiddle before you know it. Now, I've got a question, and think real hard before you answer. The day you and Maude left for the mountains, did you see anyone visit Aunt Hallie?"

There was another long silence. "Is that right?"

Kenni's nerve endings were jumping with curiosity.

"Do tell," Miss Laverne said before lapsing into another long silence.

So *that* was how she gleaned her information. She was a good listener. It was a lesson a lot of people should learn.

After a short discussion of the merits of mayonnaise versus Miracle Whip, Miss Laverne finally got off the phone.

"I personally like Miracle Whip," Kenni offered, not that she was asked or that it was relevant.

"Me, too," Miss Laverne agreed. "Stanley can go off on the strangest tangents, but that's neither here nor there. He and Maude were at their cabin up in the Smoky Mountains. They just got back yesterday."

"Miss Laverne, what did he notice?" Kenni asked, trying to keep the woman on task.

"Let's see. He told me he saw Walter go in her back door that day. He's pretty sure about the date because they were packing to leave. He heard about Hallie getting killed, but until I tweaked his memory, he'd forgotten about seeing Walter. Poor man, he's been having a few senior moments lately, but I guess that's understandable—he has his hands full with Maude. She's not in good health."

"Walter? Are you talking about my ex-husband, Walter?"

"One and the same."

Walter? No way! He couldn't be a murderer, could he? There had to be a logical reason for his visit to Aunt Hallie. But what? She wasn't one of his drinking buddies.

She did, however, own a valuable piece of property. And Walter had a vested interest in making sure that real estate project went forward. Jeez, oh jeez, oh man! Not Walter! Not the man she'd pledged to love forever. Did that make her the worst judge of character on the planet?

Kenni knew that every one of those thoughts flitted across her face because when she glanced at Win, he was frowning.

"I think we should make another visit to the sheriff," he suggested.

Damned straight, and the GBI, and the FBI, and the CIA… Okay, slow down, girl. Deep breath…one, two, three, another deep breath.

"You're right," Kenni agreed, then gave Miss Laverne a hug. "As distressing as this news is, I appreciate it. Hopefully, we can clear Bubba Gene's name."

The elderly woman reciprocated with a squeeze. "I've always liked that boy. His mother was a real lady, one of the best."

THE SHERIFF'S OFFICE HAD seen better days. Its heyday was somewhere around the end of the Civil War. The last remodel must've been part of the Depression Era make-work program. In fact, it looked more like a dungeon than a cop shop, Kenni thought, seeing the place as she imagined Win must be seeing it. They made their way through a rabbit warren of small offices and even more diminutive cubicles.

"Hey, sweetie. Tell me you have good news," Dave said, embracing Kenni as only a favorite uncle would.

"And, Win, good to see you." The two men shook hands. "Have a seat. I'm hopin' you have something good to tell me." Dave indicated two well-worn leather chairs in front of his desk.

"I don't know that I'd call it good," Kenni said with a sigh. "But we did go over to Miss Laverne's house."

Dave propped his elbows on his desk. "What did you find out?"

"We, uh, she, uh…"

Win took over the explanation. "She called Stanley Cook, one of Hallie's neighbors. He's been out of town since before the body was discovered, but he said he was packing the car that day and remembers seeing Walter Harrington go into the house."

"Damn. After the murder, we tried to find the Cooks to interview them, but they'd already left for their mountain cabin and they don't have a phone up there. I didn't know they were back. Why didn't Stanley call me?"

"I asked that exact question," Win said. "According to Miss Laverne, he simply didn't make the connection, at least not until she tweaked his memory."

"Son of a gun!" Dave exclaimed with a sheepish expression. "I hate to say it, but I never liked Walter. He's too slick for my taste."

Dave's observation merited applause. Too bad Kenni hadn't noticed Walter's character deficiency before she'd said "I do."

Dave picked up the phone and punched in some numbers. "Sam, would you come in here, please. There's something I want you to hear." The sheriff hung up and pushed his chair away from the desk. "Sam's my best detective, so I want him involved. How about I get you something cold to drink? We might be here a while."

Truer words were never spoken. The order of the day was a brainstorming session about scrutinizing one of the town's leading citizens without creating too much heartburn.

Fortunately, the police had obtained some DNA from the scene. So now their problem was how to snooker Walter into making a donation. There were two options: following him around to see if he discarded anything useful, or having Kenni invite him to her house.

"No way," Win objected.

"Wait," Kenni said, putting her hand on his arm. "I think it'll work. I found some of his old books and stuff in the attic. I was going to throw it away but I could ask him to come over and pick it up." She grinned. "It'll work, I know it will."

"If you're dead set on doing this, I plan to be in the other room." Win put his arms across his chest.

"My deputies and I will be outside just in case something goes wrong," Dave assured her.

"No kidding! I don't want to be alone with a murderer. Not

that I haven't been alone with him before. A lot, in fact." Kenni frowned, thinking about her intimate relationship with a possible felon.

Why did she have such abominable taste in men? She looked at Win. Well, at least her taste had improved—considerably.

Chapter Twenty-Eight

Although Kenni's attic was stifling, she attacked the chore of boxing Walter's possessions with the passion of a dervish. She'd spent too many years feeling sorry for him.

Before she knew it, she had three boxes of knickknacks, books and old clothes stacked by the front door. She'd prefer to toss the crap out to the curb, but that wouldn't provide the saliva sample they needed. So, like it or not, she was about to play hostess.

"How are you doing?" Win asked, kissing her neck.

He'd been such a trouper, braving the attic and supplying the muscle power. "Not bad. I want to get this over with."

"I can't blame you. Remember, I'll be in the kitchen, so don't let him in there."

That wouldn't be a problem. In all the years they'd been married, the only time Walter had entered the kitchen was to snag a beer.

"Here he comes." Kenni didn't panic often, but wow, her heart was beating a mile a minute.

"Don't worry. If things get dicey, simply scream, and I'll come running," Win assured her before disappearing through the door, and not a minute too soon. The doorbell rang.

Showtime.

"Walter, come in." She opened the screen door.

"Looks like you're trying to get rid of me again," her ex said, eyeing the pile of boxes.

"Although we're divorced, we should try to be civil," Kenni responded. "Would you like some iced tea?" She'd rather serve him strychnine, but it was time to think like Nancy Drew.

Walter wandered into the living room, fingering everything in sight.

Get your hands off my things.

"I suppose I could stay around for a cold drink."

"Fine, I'll get it." Kenni scampered off to the kitchen. The minute he left, she planned to take a long, hot shower. Lord in heaven, she felt dirty.

Win put his arms around her, brushing her mouth with a kiss. "You're doing fine. Take a deep breath and think calming thoughts."

"You mean like killing him?"

"That works."

To facilitate their evidence gathering, Kenni had prepared a tray with two glasses and a pitcher. No cookies, no treats, absolutely nothing that would delay Walter's departure. All she wanted to do was obtain some spit. Then she'd kick his worthless behind out the door.

"We have it!" she exclaimed. After Walter left, Kenni carefully poured out the remainder of the tea and placed the glass in a Ziploc bag. She proudly displayed her prize to Dave and his detective. "How long will it take to process?"

"It'll be at least a week, probably more like two. And that's putting a rush on it. We have to send it off to Atlanta," Sam told her.

"Seriously?" That wasn't the way it worked on TV. "So you can't do anything until you get some evidence, huh?"

"That's our process. We're eager to close this case, too. So don't worry," Dave reassured her.

Somehow that seemed easier said than done.

LIFE SLOWLY RESUMED its normal cadence as Win tried to decide the best way to approach Bubba Gene. Although he wanted Walter to be found guilty, something was out of kilter, and he intended to find out what it was. But he wasn't ready to tell Kenni about his plan. At least not yet.

"Hey, big guy. Do you want to go with me to the Temptee Freeze? I'll treat you to a milk shake."

"That'd be right nice. I thank ya very much. Let me put my mop away and wash my hands. Mama always told me to clean my hands before I ate anything. Do you do that?" Bubba asked.

"I certainly do," Win agreed.

WIN WAITED until his new friend had almost finished his strawberry milk shake before he broached the subject.

"Can you tell me what happened to Aunt Hallie?" Win was experienced in questioning reluctant witnesses; however, in this situation he had to be extra careful.

Bubba Gene ducked his head and tied a knot in the straw.

"Cross my heart, I promise I won't say anything."

"Mr. Win, I'm in bad trouble, aren't I?"

"Perhaps not. We'll have to see how things go," Win responded as honestly as he could.

Bubba Gene was quiet for such a long time, Win was afraid he had clammed up.

"That day I was cuttin' grass, you know like I always do on Saturdays before I go to the movies." He paused and looked at Win. "Do you like Ariel?"

"Yes, I do. Very much." Win tried to redirect the conversation. "Now back to the day at Aunt Hallie's place."

"I heard this racket, and then people were yelling. So I thought I should go see what was happenin'. I was afraid Aunt Hallie was in trouble. Would you get me another milk shake?"

"Sure. What flavor?"

"Chocolate."

"I'll be right back." This was going to take patience, but Win wasn't about to quit.

Bubba Gene finished the second shake but remained silent. Win knew a stall when he saw one.

"So back to Aunt Hallie, what happened next?"

Bubba Gene picked at the edge of his paper cup. "I went into the kitchen, and there she was, all bloody and everything. I didn't do it, really I didn't." A single tear ran down his cheek.

"I know."

"Really, you don't think I did somethin' bad?" There was hope in his voice.

"No, I don't think you did anything bad."

Win's assurance was enough incentive for Bubba Gene to continue. "I squatted down next to her and tried to keep all that blood from coming out, but I couldn't, it just kept comin' and comin'. Then the maid came in and started screaming. I tried to get her to help, but she yelled louder. She was mad at me. I thought about runnin' but I couldn't leave Aunt Hallie."

"Did you see who was in the kitchen with her?"

"Nope. Can we go back to Miss Kenni's now?"

Win realized that was all the information he was going to get from Bubba Gene, but he had to ask the final question. "Could her visitor have been Mr. Walter Harrington?"

"Oh no, he did come by that day, but I talked to Aunt Hallie after he left."

Well, damn!

Chapter Twenty-Nine

While Bubba Gene and Win were busy blowing Kenni's theory about the murder out of the water, she was pondering the garden party. At dinner the night before she'd asked Win if he still wanted to attend. Not surprisingly, he had answered her with a kiss.

Damn—she loved the way that man thought.

Then she remembered the bet—the wager that had brought him into her life. That dirty dog wanted to go so he could win. After she'd huffed and puffed, and generally acted like a brat, Win had the audacity to laugh.

"WHAT DID YOU BUY?" Raylene took the shopping bag out of Kenni's hands. "My curiosity is killing me."

"Me, too." Toolie was jumping up and down, waiting for Kenni to display her purchase.

After she had succumbed to Win's powers of persuasion, Kenni's next thought was typically female; what was she going to wear? Most of her wardrobe ran toward jeans and T-shirts, with a couple of skirts and blouses thrown in for baby showers and Tupperware parties.

Against her better judgment, Kenni went on a pilgrimage to buy dress-up clothes. The garden party was an event she'd always managed to avoid, so she was pretty clueless about the appropriate attire.

"What do you think?" She pulled a dress from a glossy shopping bag. The gauzy fabric looked like an Impressionist painting with a palette of pale pink swirling toward a soft rose.

The saleswoman had assured her it was the perfect outfit. But she'd been working on commission. Now Kenni was about to get the truth from a couple of ladies who were known for being painfully honest.

"That's beautiful," Toolie murmured.

"Oh, honey. You're gonna knock his socks off," Raylene gushed. "It's a dress made for royalty."

That was exactly what Kenni wanted to hear. "You're sure it's okay?"

Raylene held it up to Kenni. "This little number is more than okay. It has the Raylene Yarborough stamp of approval. And we're gonna come over to help you get dressed."

"Tell you what, I'll bring my clothes to the salon and you guys can work your miracle here." Kenni wanted Win's eyes to bug out when he saw her.

Raylene gave her one of those "what are you up to?" looks before she smiled. Yep, her friend wasn't fooled.

THE DAY of the garden party dawned clear and gorgeous. It was seasonally warm, but not stifling, and even better, there wasn't a thunderstorm in sight. Too bad Kenni wasn't feeling quite as dazzling. At the last minute, she'd realized she'd rather go to a tractor pull than get all gussied up and hang out in someone's backyard, regardless of their horticultural prowess.

"You're looking gorgeous. Monet couldn't have done it better," Win said, distributing soft kisses up and down her collarbone. "I love you," he whispered.

Whew! That was the exact reaction Kenni was going for. It was time to buy a closetful of frilly dresses.

"You look pretty good yourself." She couldn't get past how handsome her date was in his exquisitely tailored suit, snow-white shirt and red silk tie.

"Shall we go?"

"I suppose we have to. Although I can think of some other things we could do," Kenni said with a wink.

"Don't tempt me. Anna Belle would be mad if we were a no-show."

"Yeah," Kenni agreed, somewhat reluctantly.

WIN HAD DECIDED TO HOLD OFF telling anyone about his conversation with Bubba Gene, especially Kenni. He wasn't sure how she would react. A couple of days wouldn't hurt, and he really didn't want to ruin the party.

"How are my two favorite people?" Anna Belle asked, giving Kenni a hug. "Are you having fun?"

"Of course." Kenni smiled at her aunt. If Win hadn't been privy to her muttering, *he* would have thought she was enjoying herself.

"Miss Anna Belle, this is wonderful. You've outdone yourself. Shall we have a toast?" Win held up his champagne flute. "To the two prettiest women in town."

Anna Belle blushed as she raised her glass. "You're right about Kenni being beautiful."

"You're both gorgeous."

Anna Belle gave him a hug, and Kenni knew from Win's expression that the spontaneous show of affection was unexpected. He never said much about his childhood, so she had to wonder what it had been like. She knew his parents didn't spend much time in the country.

What did that mean? Her fertile imagination could dredge

up all kinds of scenarios ranging from them being on the FBI's Ten Most Wanted list to them conducting a money-laundering scheme.

Kenni's musings about Win's family took a back seat when she spied Walter with a voluptuous brunette on his arm.

"Are you watching Walter?" Win whispered, causing goose bumps to scamper up her spine.

"Uh-huh," she murmured. "Look at him. Not a care in the world. How could he commit a murder and then act like…that?" She waved a hand in the air. "And how could I have married him?"

Win pulled her toward a bench at the edge of the garden. "Let's sit down," he urged. "We need to talk. You have to remember he's only a suspect. At the moment, everything is alleged." Win was tempted to tell her about Bubba Gene, but decided to speak to the sheriff first.

"Spoken like a true lawyer. Alleged, my rear—you know he did it. I know he did it, and he sure knows he did it," Kenni proclaimed with a pout. "The only thing I can't figure out is why. Was it an accident or did he intend to kill her? I hope to God it was an accident."

That did it. He had to tell her what was happening, but he wanted some privacy to do it. "Are you about ready to go home?"

"Sure," she agreed. However, before they made it to the door, they ran into Maizie and Clay.

"Hey, guys. When we find Liza and Charlie we're heading to the pub for a beer. I've had about all the canapés I can stand. Want to join us?" Maizie asked.

Actually that didn't sound half-bad. The company would be fun, and a cold beer sounded mighty fine. Plus, it gave Win a good excuse to procrastinate.

"What do you think?" Kenni looked to him for confirmation.

"I'm game. Let's thank our hostess and beat feet."

Kenni grinned.

"I'm right behind you," she assured him, pushing Win toward the group of middle-aged women who were hostesses for the shindig.

Chapter Thirty

"Kenni, sweetie, it's Uncle Dave. I'd like for you and Win to come down to the office." It was Sunday, and Dave didn't normally work on weekends, so she knew it was important.

"Is this about the DNA?"

"Uh-huh. You guys need to come on down."

"Is it good or bad?"

"Thirty minutes?"

He was doing the strong silent cop thing. "We'll be there shortly."

She disconnected and punched in Win's cell number. He was out doing God only knew what. Although their evening had been wonderful, he was acting strange today. "Uncle Dave called and wants us to come down to the station. It's about the DNA," she told him when he answered.

"I'll pick you up in a few minutes."

The courthouse wasn't more than five minutes by car from Kenni's house, ten if you encountered a funeral procession. This time the trip seemed interminable.

"I'm nervous," Kenni said, twisting her fingers. "What if I've been accusing Walter of something horrible and he's innocent?" she wailed. "That would make me feel like dog poop. And if he really did it, that's even worse."

"Kenni." Win pulled over to the side of the road. "I have to tell you something." He turned in the seat to look at her. "I've been trying to figure out how to say this, but I'm a coward. Two days ago I talked to Bubba Gene. He told me that Walter was at Aunt Hallie's the day of the murder, and that she was alive when he left."

"What?"

"Walter didn't kill Hallie. I'm sure the DNA will prove it." He picked up her hand. "We'll get through this, I promise."

"Oh, God."

UNCLE DAVE OFFERED coffee but Kenni was too upset to put a thing in her stomach. Her mouth was so dry she couldn't say a word if her life depended on it.

Win apparently wasn't working under the same limitation. "Sheriff, sir. I have some new information." He then told Dave about his conversation with Bubba Gene.

"I questioned him, and he didn't tell me any of that," Dave said with a rueful expression.

"I guess I lucked into asking him the right question. So I'm assuming the DNA didn't match?"

"Yep." Dave paced from the window to his desk. "Hell of a mess, isn't it? Now we're back to square one. I don't believe Bubba Gene did anything and I suspect the district attorney is on the same page. I can't tell you any specifics, but we're developing some new ideas."

LATER IN THE EVENING Kenni and Win were snuggled on the couch while Miss Priss claimed her favorite spot. His lap. Somehow along the way, Kenni's cat had decided Win was one of her favorite humans.

"What are we going to do now?"

Win hesitated before speaking. "*We're* not going to do anything. It's time to leave it to the police."

Kenni sat up and gave Win one of those looks. "Even though

Walter didn't kill Aunt Hallie, I believe he's the one who has been threatening me, and I intend to prove it. If I don't, I'll never feel safe again."

"We have to trust in the system."

Kenni snorted. "Do you seriously believe justice will be served? An innocent old lady was killed, someone not only shot at us but they also tried to torch my business, and the police don't have a shred of evidence. Do you honestly think we can rely on the system?"

Win was an attorney—he had to believe in the law. Unfortunately, he was afraid he was about to lose this argument, and that was before Liza called, and Kenni smirked at him.

Her attitude didn't bode well for Win's case. "I'll bite. What did she say?" he asked, even though he didn't want to hear the answer.

"Liza said that Charlie had dinner with his developer friend from Atlanta and guess what the guy said."

Win was no dummy. He knew when to throw in the towel.

"Beats me."

"According to him, Walter assured them that he's taking care of the problem. I'd bet the farm the *problem* is me. It makes sense. I think, deep down, he's always been angry that I was willing to stand up to his mother and he wasn't. And now he sees me as a threat to his land deal."

Win couldn't argue with that line of reasoning. "So what do you have in mind?"

KENNI KNEW THE MINUTE she'd won. "Let's assume we have two separate crimes, the murder and the threats. And let's further presume that Walter is the person who has been terrorizing me. I think we should go at this from a business angle. Let's scare the truth out of him."

"How do you intend to do that?"

"We'll have Charlie talk to his friend. That development

company would not be pleased with the bad publicity I'm willing to stir up."

Win sighed. "If you accuse Walter of something without proof, he can sue you and win."

"I don't plan for it to get that far. My ex is *not* a brave man. He hasn't stood up to Beatrice the Beast in his entire life. We'll let the big guy in Atlanta do our dirty work for us. All it will take is a few well-placed words and good old Walter will fold like a cheap lawn chair."

Chapter Thirty-One

Two days later, Kenni and Raylene were getting ready for the Permanently Yours grand reopening when the bell on the front door welcomed a visitor.

"We're in the back," Kenni yelled, expecting to see Win with a box of Krispy Kremes. Instead, she looked up and saw Walter. Yikes!

"Raylene." Kenni didn't know what else to say.

"I see him, and I have my cell ready to call 911," Raylene muttered.

"Walter, what do you want?"

"To talk to you. In private."

Raylene moved toward Kenni in a show of support.

"Raylene stays. You have five minutes to say what you have to say. Then I want you out of here."

Obviously distraught, Walter ran his fingers through his thinning hair. The poor old boy was feeling guilty, and wasn't that too bad. He'd made his bed and now he was in for a prickly lie down.

"Kenni, I, uh, I…"

"Five minutes." She held up five fingers. "Your time is running out so you'd better hurry."

"I'm sorry."

"I beg your pardon?"

"I'm sorry." He hung his head. "I didn't intend to hurt you, honestly I didn't. I started the fire and shot at you—but it was just to scare you. I wanted you to butt out. This real-estate deal was my one chance to get away from Magnolia Bluffs."

Kenni really, really wanted to beat the stuffing out of the jerk, but somehow she managed to maintain some semblance of civility. "So you're admitting to the arson, the shooting, the threatening notes *and* the vandalism?"

"Yeah," Walter mumbled, as he pushed his hands into his pockets. "If I pay for your cleanup and buy you a bunch of new stuff, would you consider getting me off the hook with the Atlanta boys?"

He looked so contrite, Kenni was tempted to help him, but not quite yet. Regardless of his show of remorse, he'd committed a number of felonies. His career was probably the least of his problems. Uncle Dave would not be amused.

"So why did you focus on me instead of Liza or Maizie?" That question had bothered her from the very beginning.

"Because I know you better."

"You know me. You bet your sweet rear you know me. We were married!" Kenni could barely contain the screech that was itching to escape. "Here's the deal. I'll get you out of this mess, at least with your business partners, on two conditions. You never talk to me or bother me again. If you see me walking down the street, you'd better hightail it to other side. In fact, I think you'd be happier if you relocated to Atlanta. And second, you have to confess to Uncle Dave."

"I have to tell the sheriff?" he whined.

"Yes. They say that confession is good for the soul." Kenni put her hands on her hips. That condition was nonnegotiable. Dave would make sure Walter faced up to his responsibilities.

He was obviously trying to decide whether he could live with her ultimatum, then he capitulated.

"Okay. I'll go see him right now."

"That's a good decision."

"You go, girl," Raylene exclaimed, as Walter trudged out the door. "Give me five," she said, raising her hand in celebration.

"I HAVE SOME REALLY good news." Kenni had waited until after dinner, dessert, and some good old-fashioned lovin' before she broke the news.

"What?" he asked, nuzzling her neck and generally distracting them both.

"I talked to Walter today."

He sat up so fast he almost dumped her off the bed. "You did what?"

"Walter came by the shop and confessed to pulling all the stunts against me," Kenni said with a smirk. It wasn't very ladylike but she couldn't help herself.

"He confessed?"

"Yep, and he's gonna talk to Uncle Dave."

"I'll be damned. He said he'd leave you alone?"

"Yeah." Kenni told him all about the conversation.

"THAT'S GREAT NEWS," he said, stacking his arms behind his head. "Now let's talk about us." Kenni didn't seem very enthusiastic about this conversation, so Win decided to put her at ease. And that, of course, required some kisses—one of his favorite pastimes.

He had some life-changing plans in mind. He'd been weighing alternatives for some time now. Although it was looking more and more like the charges against Bubba Gene would be dropped due to lack of evidence, it was obvious the town could use a good defense attorney. Add that professional opportunity to the miracles of modern travel and technology, and Win felt he could work part-time with the D.C. office, while spending most of the year in Magnolia Bluffs.

Heck, Wharton and Whittaker could even open an Atlanta office.

"I love you," he declared. Win almost asked her to marry him, but hesitated. This was the one-and-only time he ever intended to ask for anyone's hand, so he wanted to do it right. And that meant having a ring in his pocket and a viable relocation plan in place.

"I love you, too," she answered, snuggling closer.

He tweaked her nose, then followed up with an erotic nibble on her ear. "Colby called and said there's a glitch with one of my cases," he said. "So I have to go back to D.C. tomorrow. With Walter out of the picture, I feel a whole lot better leaving you alone." Then he did some more delightful things to her neck and collarbone. "I'll probably be gone at least a week." Talking and kissing was taxing even to Win's vaunted ability to multitask.

"I want you to come up to meet my friends."

"I can do that." After she started unbuttoning his shirt he wasn't sure what she had agreed to do.

IT WAS TRUE; there was a problem with one of his cases. However, the bigger reason for the trip was to make plans for his future. Two days into his negotiation with Colby, Win realized the operation would take much longer than he expected. They weren't exactly disassembling their law firm; however, they were undertaking a major reorganization. Fortunately, they weren't in the middle of any high-profile cases so the primary players had the time to concentrate on the firm's new hierarchy.

"Are you sure you want to do this?" Colby asked. They were at the Hair of the Hound enjoying a beer.

"I'm absolutely positive," Win declared, shooting his partner a grin. "I'm in love."

"Man!" Colby shook his head. "And to think I'm responsible. I guess that means I have to be your best man." He clapped Win on the back. "Never thought I'd see the day."

"Neither did I," Win admitted. "You should try it."

Colby pushed back his stool. "Not me, buddy. By the way, when's your fiancée coming up?"

Win studied his beer before replying. "Actually, I haven't officially asked her. I'm waiting for the right moment."

Colby glared at his friend. "Let me get this straight. You're turning your professional life upside down, and you haven't asked her to marry you?"

"When you put it that way, it sounds pretty stupid, doesn't it?"

"Yeah. Dumber than dirt."

Win knew Colby was right and that made him really nervous. The predicted week had stretched to almost three. He talked to her almost every day, but it wasn't the same. He was antsy to get back to Georgia.

"I suggest you get a ring on that girl's finger," Colby said with a frown. "For a smart guy, you have mush for brains."

Chapter Thirty-Two

"Have you heard from that handsome honey of yours?" Although Joynelle Tucker asked the question, everyone in the salon stopped to listen.

"Sure, I've talked to him. In fact, I'm going to Georgetown for the weekend. He's having a party and wants me to meet his friends," Kenni replied. Since she didn't know exactly where their relationship was going, she wasn't tempted to elaborate. He'd said he loved her, but they hadn't discussed anything permanent.

"That's right nice. Did you get a new dress?" Viola Horatio asked, but before Kenni could answer, she continued her questions. "Have you heard anything new about the murder?"

Kenni was about to respond when Laverne Hightower rendered everyone speechless. Raylene dropped her scissors.

"I've been cogitating about this, and I don't know why I didn't think of it before. Did you know that Crumpy and Hallie Rule were sweethearts back before the war?"

Please, God, she wasn't talking about the Civil War again.

"The war?" Kenni asked.

"World War II."

"Crumpy and Aunt Hallie dated?" Kenni hated to sound obtuse, but that didn't make any sense.

"Yep. Don't know why those two never got hitched. I suspect it had something to do with their families. That and the fact that they fought all the time. Age didn't improve their dispositions, none at all." Laverne cackled in glee. "It was all a big secret. Only Hallie's very best friends knew. Even her family was kept in the dark. If you want my opinion, Crumpy's your guy."

Good grief! How had *that* bit of information escaped the attention of the rumor-mongers? And had Uncle Dave discovered any of it during his investigation?

"WE HAVE TO TALK, so why don't you guys meet me at the Dew Drop Inn," Kenni said without preamble.

"Yes, ma'am," Liza agreed with a chuckle. "Any particular time your majesty would like us to appear?" she asked.

"Can it, cuz, and let's make it five o'clock."

"Now you have my curiosity up. We'll be there."

The Dew Drop Inn wasn't their normal stompin' ground, but the tavern seemed like the perfect place to discuss murder and mayhem.

"I ordered margaritas and nachos," Kenni informed her cousins when they arrived.

"Merciful heavens, I hope this discussion doesn't require tequila," Maizie said, dropping her purse into an empty chair.

"Me, too," Liza agreed with a frown.

Kenni waited until the waitress delivered their drinks before she proceeded. "Here's the deal. I want to go out to Crumpy Hardaway's place to do some investigating."

"No way! You *are* nuts," Maizie exclaimed.

Considering Maizie was always ready for an adventure, that wasn't a good sign, but Kenni forged ahead.

"You'll never guess what Laverne Hightower told us." After Kenni finished her story, it took several minutes for the cousins to process the new information.

"So what do you want us to do?" Liza asked.

"And why aren't you going to Uncle Dave with this?" Maizie chimed in.

"I made such a huge deal about Walter that I don't think Uncle Dave will believe me. Not unless I have something more to go on than Laverne Hightower's word. You remember that he and Laverne aren't exactly buddies."

"Isn't that the truth! She'd just as soon gut him with an oyster knife as look at him," Maizie agreed. "So what do you want us to do?"

"Let's go out there right now."

"Right now?" Liza squeaked.

"Yes, right now. It's five o'clock and his worthless grandsons will be at the bar."

"There is that," Maizie agreed. "Let's do it." She picked up her purse, ready for action.

"ARE WE ABSOLUTELY SURE this is a good idea?" Liza asked, as their car fell into a pothole the size of an eight-person hot tub.

Even Kenni was having doubts about the wisdom of this little jaunt. "Look out," she yelled, as Maizie drove them straight into another abyss.

"I think we've found the right address." Liza indicated a clearing where several rusted trailers sat amid a sea of derelict cars and ancient appliances.

"I've seen junk farms, but this one takes the cake." Maizie hit the automatic locks. "Unless St. Peter comes out of that place with an engraved invitation, we're not getting out of this car."

"Ye gods, that dog looks rabid," Liza screamed. The canine in question had jumped up and was going nose-to-nose with Kenni through the window.

"Yikes!" Kenni jerked away, almost strangling herself on the seat belt.

"This wasn't such a good idea, huh?" Kenni hated to admit it, but this appeared to be another in a long line of mistakes.

"Look, there's Crumpy." Maizie indicated a wizened old man who was stalking across the beaten-down grass.

"That man fell out of the ugly tree and hit every branch on the way down." The pithy remark came from Liza.

Life hadn't been kind to Crumpy Hardaway.

"What do you gals want?" he demanded, thumping on the window.

"Do we roll down the window?" Kenni asked.

"No!"

"Yes," Maizie said, countermanding her sister.

Kenni compromised by cracking open the window. "We want to talk to you about Hallie Rule's death."

Apparently she'd uttered the magic words. With a huff, a puff and a grimace, he conceded. "Come on in, if ya have to. Makes no never mind to me." With that he marched toward the trailer. The dog gave a whimper and followed him.

"Are you really going in there?" Liza asked, looking a smidge green.

Kenni hesitated. This was her big idea, but was she willing to risk dying? That was unlikely, though, wasn't it? "If we want to get to the truth, we have to gut up and talk to him. Right?"

Maizie nodded reluctantly.

"There are three of us and one of him. What can he do?" Liza said, although she didn't say it with much conviction.

"Let's go." Kenni hopped out of the car. She hoped her cousins would follow, and she wasn't disappointed.

Maizie walked around the front of the car and linked arms with Kenni and Liza. "There's safety in numbers. Let's do it."

Together the three marched into the lion's den—aka Crumpy's trailer.

"Sit yourself down if you want. I'll tell you right off I don't have nothin' to say." He was ensconced in a massive recliner with the dog at his feet.

Kenni sat gingerly on an ancient couch that was repaired with duct tape. Liza was apparently trying to find something wooden to sit on, but failing that she joined her cousin. Maizie plopped down beside them.

"I already talked to the sheriff. Told him he'd better leave my family alone or I'd have his badge." Crumpy slapped his knee. "That's a good one. Knew his father, ya know. That old man was as stubborn as his kid. Dave's a purty good sheriff, but that's neither here nor there. All my family's got alibis for each other. He ain't got nothin' on us."

Kenni had to wonder what the "nothing" was. Did that mean Crumpy was responsible for Aunt Hallie's death? Or was he covering for one of his relatives? What would Nancy Drew do?

Nancy would go straight for the jugular. "I understand you were in love with Hallie. Why didn't you get married?"

He appeared shocked, but quickly recovered. "Where'd you hear that, girlie?" He didn't quite shout, but it was apparent her question bothered him.

"Everyone at the beauty salon knows." Thanks to Laverne Hightower, that was the truth.

Crumpy closed his eyes as if to go back in time. "I loved that girl. She was the purtiest thing I ever seen. We started sneakin' around way back before the war, and then I was drafted." He rubbed his forehead. "When I got back she was married. Her old man knew we were sweet on each other, so he made sure she was off the market. I never got over her. You don't forget the first person you love." He was deep in thought.

Kenni felt bad for him and her cousins looked equally sympathetic. "So, do you know anything that could help us find the person who hurt her?"

The old man shook his head. He had tears in his eyes. "Might as well tell you. My conscience is makin' itchy. My boys don't understand. They say just keep my mouth shut and it'll go away, but I didn't want the memory of Hallie to go away. I didn't mean to hurt her."

Kenni's mouth dropped open. He was going to confess.

Crumpy's story was a strange mixture of *Romeo and Juliet* and *Bonnie and Clyde*. Their love affair had been thwarted, but as neighbors they'd maintained a distant but amicable relationship. Until the specter of big money popped up. Then everything went to hell in a handbasket.

"I went over there to talk to her. All I wanted was a nice, civilized powwow. Damnation, she had more money than she could ever use and we're poor as church mice. The way I figured, we should split the money evenly. But no way. She wanted it all."

He paused to gather his thoughts. "She started screaming at me. Then she tried to hit me with a fireplace poker. I shoved her and that's when it happened. She wasn't none too sure on her feet, so she fell and hit her head. I checked her pulse and there wasn't none. Damn, those head wounds bleed a lot." By that time, tears were flowing down his weathered cheeks. "I never meant to hurt her. I loved her."

It was an unfortunate accident, not a murder. Wasn't *that* something?

KENNI WAS ON HER CELL calling Uncle Dave before Crumpy's dog stopped chasing their car. Now the cousins were back at the Dew Drop Inn having a debriefing session over a plate of nachos and a fresh pitcher of margaritas.

"Can you believe he confessed?" Liza shook her head in disbelief. "Normal people don't do things like that."

"Crumpy's not normal," Maizie asserted, pouring another round of drinks. "What kind of charges do you think he'll face?"

"Boy, I don't know." Kenni shrugged. "All I know is that I'm thrilled the charges against Bubba Gene are going to be dropped. I feel sorry for Crumpy. He really did love Aunt Hallie and it was an accident."

Liza and Maizie nodded their agreement.

"Do you think we're going to have to find him an attorney?" Maizie asked.

"Maybe I can talk Win into representing him." Kenni's giggle was a combination of tequila overload and a vision of cool, sophisticated Win taking on the king of the rednecks.

"Speaking of your handsome boyfriend," Maizie said, crunching on another chip. "Tell me exactly what he said about this shindig you're going to."

"He didn't tell me squat, other than he was giving a party and I should dress up."

"Hmm," Liza murmured.

"So, what are his intentions?" That question came from Maizie. The girl was nosy beyond belief. "Are you going to marry him and move to, uh…Washington?" She mentioned the name of the nation's capital in the same tone she would have used to describe a toxic waste dump. To make matters worse, Liza nodded in agreement.

"What's with you two? No wonder Yankees think we're bumpkins."

Not inclined to let someone else have the last word, Maizie continued the inquisition. "Yankees, spankees. That doesn't answer our question about a wedding."

"We haven't discussed marriage, so I think it's a bit premature to select bridesmaids' dresses. And that's the last I'm going to say on the matter. For now, anyway," Kenni said with a giggle.

Chapter Thirty-Three

The day before she left for Georgetown was a whirlwind of activity. Kenni was in the salon's storeroom checking the inventory of shampoo when her cell phone rang. Was it in her pocket? Of course not.

Was it on the front counter? More than likely.

That would have been okay if she hadn't tripped over a box and landed on her derriere. So once again, Win's voice found its way to her voice mail.

"Hi, sweetheart. Just calling to see what you're doing and to find out what time your flight gets in." There was a pause and she could hear conversation in the background. "I've gotta go. Talk to you later. Love ya."

His voice was a perfect combination of a velvety baritone with just a little Southern drawl mixed in. No wonder he could mesmerize a jury.

No sooner did she hit the disconnect button when the cell chirped again. This time it was Maizie.

"What time do we need to leave for the airport?"

"Early, really early. How about four o'clock?"

"Great, I love predawn travel." That was the biggest lie in the world. Maizie was *not* a morning person. "Have you talked to that handsome man of yours lately?"

"Not for a day or two," Kenni replied with a sigh. "I just got another voice mail."

She missed him like crazy. In fact, Kenni couldn't wait to get her hands on him. For sure, there was gonna be some kissin', cuddling and other good stuff in her very near future.

THE ALARM CLOCK JARRED HER out of a deep sleep. Darn, she was in the middle of hot, wild sex.

"Sheesh," Kenni muttered, hitting the snooze button. She was about to dive under her pillow when she got a whiff of fresh-brewed coffee. It was the elixir of the gods, cure of all ills—wonderful caffeine-laden java, guaranteed to give her a kick start. Thank God for automatic coffeepots.

Kenni had just finished zipping the last bag when Maizie barged into the kitchen.

"I'd kill for a cup of coffee," she said, rummaging through the cupboard for a cup.

Kenni would have laughed at her cousin's desperation; however, she felt the same way.

"Let's get rolling. We have at least an hour's drive and that doesn't account for traffic." Maizie grabbed the largest suitcase and headed to the car. "Close to the city, the traffic jams start around five o'clock."

Unfortunately, those words proved to be prophetic.

Their undoing, however, was a jackknifed semi on I-75 that backed up traffic for miles.

"Do you think all these people get up at this ungodly time every morning?" Maizie complained, looking over the sea of cars.

"The next exit we creep up to, I'm getting off this highway. You'll miss your flight if we don't get movin'," she declared, taking stock of the situation. "In fact, I'm going to drive up the shoulder to that next exit. Watch for cops," Maizie instructed, seconds before she pulled onto the shoulder.

"This is so illegal it hurts." Kenni held on to the armrest and prayed they wouldn't get arrested or even worse, killed. "It's a good thing you have a 4x4. That concrete median you ran over would've wrecked anything else."

Maizie responded with a grin and a wink. "Hang on, you're not gonna be late."

Miraculously, they made it to the airport with a few minutes to spare. After a delay at security, Kenni got to her gate in the nick of time.

"You'd better run for it, honey, they're about to close the door," the ticket taker yelled as Kenni charged down the Jetway.

She dashed into the cabin seconds before the flight attendant slammed the door closed. Traveling sure was stressful.

KENNI WAS BATTLING a bad case of nerves as she made her way through the crowd at Dulles. What was wrong with her? She loved Win and he loved her. Didn't he?

The good news was her luggage made it. The bad news was Win was a no-show.

"Miss McAllister, over here."

Kenni scanned the crowd for the owner of the voice. Much to her dismay, it came from a gaunt man with a large red-and-purple dragon tattoo on his bicep. He was holding a sign with her name on it.

She hesitated a moment, then took the plunge. "I'm Kenni McAllister. Did Mr. Whittaker send you?"

"Yes, ma'am, I'm at your service. You can call me Tommy. Do you have everything?"

Kenni nodded, unable to come up with an articulate comment.

"Let me carry your things." He didn't wait for her to answer before stacking her bags and heading to the exit. It was hard to reconcile the man's rough exterior with his amazingly elegant manners and soft Southern accent.

"I was expecting Win. Do you know why he asked you to pick me up?"

"No, ma'am, I surely don't. He told me to tell you that he had a crisis at work and that he'd see you at the house."

"Do you have a key so I can get in?" Kenni thought about asking him to drop her at a hotel.

"No, ma'am, you won't need a key. Donna's at home. Right about now, the place will be crawling with caterers and cleaners for the party tonight."

Now she really was confused. Caterers and cleaners? What happened to the little get-together she'd expected?

"Who is Donna?"

"She's Mr. Whittaker's housekeeper, and even better, she's my wife. Everyone's been running around like chickens with their heads cut off, trying to pull this party together." Tommy smiled as if he had a big secret.

Okay, she owned a designer dress and through some miracle, it had made it through the hell of airline travel; however, that was irrelevant to the misgivings Kenni was having about this party. Caterers, housekeepers—what next—a string quartet and the prince of Lichtenstein?

"Wait right here, little lady, and I'll bring the car around," Tommy instructed as he deposited her luggage on the sidewalk.

"Don't bother. I'll come with you."

"Can't do that, it wouldn't be proper. Besides, this is my job. Why don't you wait with the luggage? I'll be right back."

It was his job? Good grief! He was a chauffeur. What *had* she gotten herself into?

Kenni was so caught up in her thoughts she didn't notice the sleek black Mercedes slide to a stop in front of her.

"Miss McAllister, why don't you get in the car while I put your things in the trunk?" Tommy popped the trunk with the remote and opened the back door for her.

Win had a Mercedes and a driver? Now her curiosity was on overload. Kenni knew he was a partner in a law firm, so she'd assumed he was doing okay. However, that was a world away from being filthy rich. The way things were looking, she suspected his bank balance was in the millions.

Why would he want a small-town girl with a Wal-Mart wardrobe—especially one with such a humble beginning?

"Is Mr. Whittaker your employer?"

"He sure is," Tommy announced proudly.

"Are you his driver?" Call her curious—or more likely, just plain old nosy.

"I'm more of a handyman. I do whatever needs to be done around the house. I drive and do whatever."

The more questions Kenni asked, the more uncomfortable Tommy looked. Not that she could blame him, she sounded a bit like a prosecutor.

"He's incredibly wealthy, isn't he?"

Tommy didn't have to say a thing; his flushed cheeks were answer enough.

"I'm sorry." Kenni didn't want to make it awkward for him. After all, he wasn't the person who had skipped over some very important details—like being as wealthy as Croesus. "Do I have any other surprises to look forward to?"

"Well, ma'am, I guess that depends on how easy you are to surprise. I suspect you have some more coming." He paused before continuing. "If you want a piece of advice from a country boy, I think you should just take things as they come, and enjoy the ride. Everything will be fine, just fine. Take old Tommy's word for it. Donna will love pampering you."

Before Kenni could process that information, he changed the subject. "Have you been to D.C. before?"

She sat back and vaguely listened to Tommy's travelogue. The more Kenni tried to put the puzzle pieces together, the more certain she was they wouldn't ever fit.

He was a wealthy attorney—she owned a beauty salon.

He was a sophisticated city dweller—she loved living in a small town.

Damn, he probably ate duck paté—and her favorite food was pimento cheese.

Holy tamolcy! If she kept thinking this way, her head would start spinning like that kid's in *The Exorcist*. Unfortunately she didn't know the half of it. When Tommy stopped the car in front of an elegant Federalist mansion, she almost busted a button.

"We're here. Sit right where you are, little lady. I'll have you inside in just a minute." The speed with which Tommy jumped out of the vehicle indicated he was afraid she'd make a run for it. Smart man.

He quickly opened the door and helped her out to the sidewalk. "Let me take you in and introduce you to Donna. Then I'll come back and get the bags," he said, guiding her up the stairs to a ten-panel door topped by a cut-glass fanlight.

This was turning into a Cinderella moment. Kenni had grown up in a beautiful house, but Win's home was...what could you say other than it was palatial. And that was merely a description of the exterior. With its elegant marble foyer, spiral staircase and massive crystal chandelier, the interior was even more impressive.

Yep, Kenni had suddenly morphed into the country cousin.

"Jeez, Louise. That thing's got to be Waterford," she muttered under her breath.

A faint chuckle told her she'd committed the ultimate social faux pas. Commenting on brands was almost as gauche as flipping over a dinner plate to check the label. She turned to find Tommy with his arm around a short, chubby woman. Kenni finally managed to dredge up some semblance of dignity and extended her hand. "You must be Donna. I'm Kenni McAllister."

Instead of shaking Kenni's hand, Donna enveloped her in a hug.

"Well, if you aren't just as cute as a button."

Sheesh! Was Donna going to pinch her cheek.

"Adorable. Tommy, isn't she darling?"

What could you say to that, other than thank you?

"Come with me and I'll show you your room," Donna cooed. "You can get all settled. Then I'll bring you a snack. Mr. Win called. He wanted me to tell you he had some things to do at the office, but he'd be home as soon as possible."

"Oh, okay," Kenni said, following the housekeeper up the stairs.

"Mr. Win told me to put you in here, but if you'd prefer someplace else, I can do that, too." Donna opened the door to an elegant suite of rooms decorated in masculine shades of navy and burgundy. The décor screamed testosterone.

"No, this'll be fine." But would it really be? Kenni was having a major lapse of confidence. This was Win's environment, and she'd never in a million years fit.

"Just make yourself at home," Donna said as she and Tommy turned to leave.

That wasn't going to be easy. The house reeked of old money and New World aristocracy. Regardless of the fact that she'd had a wonderful childhood, Kenni had begun her life at the Magnolia Bluffs Mobile Home Park.

When in doubt, she called in the troops, and of course, that meant ringing up one of the cousins.

"We have to talk." Kenni didn't bother with a salutation when Liza answered.

"What's wrong?"

"Win has this mansion with a housekeeper, and a driver, and probably a full team of gardeners."

"What do you mean by a mansion?"

"I mean a frickin' mansion that has a Waterford chandelier the size of a Honda."

"In Georgetown?"

"Like duh."

"Do you know how much real estate goes for in that town?" Leave it to Liza, the über developer, to have the information at her fingertips.

"Millions, I imagine."

"Absolutely. So, you're telling me he's rich—and you're feeling out of your element."

"What should I do?" Kenni couldn't contain the wail that had been itching to break out ever since she'd laid eyes on the Whittaker digs.

There was a pause. "You're going to put your chin up and remember everything that Anna Belle and Eugenie taught you. You're a lady right down to the tips of your toes. You know how to use a fish fork."

Liza was right, by golly, she was correct. "Okay, I get it. I can do this." Kenni's confident tone was somewhat undermined by the sniffle that managed to sneak by her defenses. "He worked as my shampoo guy. How embarrassing is that?"

"It was his choice."

True. "But what do I do about him being filthy rich?"

"Enjoy it? He loves you."

"Yeah, yeah, okay. I vaguely remember him telling me he had a trust fund, so I suppose he wasn't trying to keep anything from me. That should make me feel better, right?"

"That a girl. Chin up. Remember, fish fork."

"Gotcha." A talk with one of her cousins always put a smile on her face.

Feeling much better, Kenni was preparing to unpack when Donna tapped on the door.

"I brought you some tea and sandwiches. And here's a cold bottle of wine. This should keep hunger at bay until the party. I told that boy I could do all the cooking, but he insisted on getting

a caterer," Donna said in a running monologue. "He said it would
be too much trouble. Mr. Win is such a considerate man. You
know I've worked for his family since he was little."

This seemed like the perfect opportunity to get some information about Win's folks.

"I didn't know that. What are they like?"

Donna looked as if she was trying to decide how much to
say, then she sighed. "They have a house in the south of France.
Ever since Mr. Whittaker retired that's where they spend most
of their time."

They had a house in the south of France. Wow!

"Mr. Whittaker's a nice man. I think he's the reason Mr. Win's
such a thoughtful guy." The housekeeper paused. "And far as
Mrs. Whittaker goes, let's just say she's…something else."
Donna snapped her mouth shut.

Was that a euphemism for a snob or a witch?

The housekeeper bustled around the room straightening items
that didn't need straightening. "She's always trying to fix Mr.
Win up with one of those snotty social girls. Swear to goodness,
if that woman isn't meddling, she isn't happy. Miss Kristen
usually ignores her mom. I say good for her. Now, what else can
I do for you?"

The font of information had apparently dried up.

"I don't need anything else. Thank you."

"All right," Donna said, putting her hands on her ample hips.
"Let me know if you need me, ya hear."

"Yes, ma'am."

Kenni's response prompted a chuckle from the housekeeper.
"You're as adorable as a speckled pup."

That time Kenni wasn't spared the cheek pinch.

"Why don't you go find that bathtub and take a long soak? I
left some nice bubble bath for you. Swear to goodness, you could
put half the Washington Redskins in that thing."

A bottle of wine and a hot soak sounded like heaven. Welcome to the life of the Rich and Famous.

What to do next—paint her toenails, kick back with some wine, catch a cab back to the airport? Not surprisingly, the wine option won.

The stiffly elegant décor was undoubtedly the work of a very high-priced interior decorator. It was beautiful, but it didn't reflect the man she knew intimately. In fact, the house looked like something out of *Architectural Digest.* It didn't have a lived-in look. There wasn't a litter box in sight. Miss Priss would hate it.

Win had seemed so comfortable in her home. He never denied her spoiled calico a lap when she made one of her arrogant demands. How could someone who lived in all this opulence seem so down home? And that brought her to the real question: Did she *really* know him?

Chapter Thirty-Four

"You must be Miss McAllister."

Kenni was jerked out of her musings by a Julia Roberts look-alike who glided through the open door as if she owned the world. And from the looks of her outfit, she probably did—own the world, that is.

"I'm Amelie Barrois." She picked up the wine bottle and checked the label. "It looks like Donna did it again," she sighed. Even her disparaging remark was done with a sexy French accent. "She makes a lot of mistakes, but Win darling is so terribly fond of her, he keeps her on. I always thought he should get European help. They have a much better concept of protocol and etiquette. Don't you agree?" She gave Kenni the same look of disapproval she had previously given the domestic brand of Chardonnay.

"Win and I have been inseparable for…" she gave an eloquent Gallic shrug "…forever. Our parents are old friends. I'll never forget the summer he spent at our villa in Provence. I frequently serve as his hostess. Did you know that?" Her smile hinted at something far more intimate than hostess duties.

Kenni couldn't believe what she was hearing. Win had told her about Amelie, but the way he talked about her, she was long gone from his life. This tall, busty and definitely gorgeous woman certainly didn't act like she was in the past tense.

"I'm terribly embarrassed Donna put you in this room. But to give her the benefit of the doubt, maybe Win didn't tell her." Amelie leaned forward indicating she was about to impart a secret.

"Tell me what?" A feeling of dread was seeping through Kenni's pores. The last time she'd felt like that was the day Mama didn't come home. This was not looking good.

"Well, it's something of a secret, but last night Winston and I came to an understanding." The debutante elegantly crossed her legs and continued. "I feel certain we'll be announcing our engagement within the month. It takes a considerable amount of time to prepare a wedding appropriate for our families."

Kenni appreciated how a mongoose might feel. Despite the Dolce and Gabbana outfit, this woman was nothing but a snake.

"I know you think you got rather close to my Winston. But frankly, he's like that. He didn't have the heart to tell you about us on the phone, so I decided to spare him the embarrassment. Besides, he felt he owed you a nice trip."

Amelie rose and wandered toward the bed. "Naturally, I'll have Donna move your things to the guest room." She turned to face Kenni. "I hope this hasn't been too inconvenient, but I'm sure you understand."

To say Kenni'd had a belly full of this bitch was an understatement of massive proportions. And apparently she wasn't finished talking.

"Please take as long as you want to dress. Donna will take care of your suitcases. I'll be downstairs going over the last-minute preparations with the caterer." With that zinger she exited.

What chutzpah. Was this a case of ultimate BS or merely the truth? Damn! Why *hadn't* Win met her at the airport?

Emergency—her rear end!

When you got down to the heart of the matter, they hadn't talked in a couple of days. And when he did leave a message he sounded distracted. It was conceivable that something had happened in that length of time—including reconciling with Miss Cotillion.

However, and it was a huge however, perhaps Donna wasn't privy to the "dump Kenni" plan. Maybe Win wanted a little farewell party before he and what's-her-name announced their joyful union.

Would anyone in their right mind make up something that outrageous? Highly unlikely—unless they were delusional, and Miss Rich Bitch looked like she was in complete control of her faculties.

OUTRAGE. EMBARRASSMENT. A dollop of insecurity.

All that was irrelevant. Obviously he'd slipped back into the sophisticated urban life and left the poor beautician in the dust.

Men—bah, humbug! They couldn't be honest about anything—money, women, jobs, anything. She was outta there!

Kenni spied the phone on the bedside table and punched in 411. When in doubt, the best thing to do was leave the party.

"I need the first flight you have to Atlanta, the quicker the better."

"I have a six forty-five. Let me see if I can get you on it." Kenni could hear the click of computer keys. "Let's see, hmm, the only ticket I have left is in business class."

"That'll be fine." It didn't matter whether it maxed out her credit card. She had to leave.

The ticket taken care of, Kenni's next chore was to find a taxi. She couldn't ask Tommy for a ride. Time was at a premium, so Kenni tossed her clothes and toiletries back into her bag, scribbled a note and left it where Win would find it.

She wasn't sneaking out with her tail between her legs. No, ma'am. Kenni's good manners forced her to drop her bags and find Donna to thank her for her hospitality.

"What do you mean you're going home? You can't leave," Donna exclaimed, wringing her hands.

"Believe me, this is for the best, honestly it is," Kenni said, trying to console the distraught housekeeper. "Amelie told me all about their engagement. There's no way I'm sticking around while they make the happy announcement." She put her arms around Donna. "It'll be fine. They won't even miss me." Tears were close to the surface, so she didn't dare say much more.

"Oh no, honey. That's not true." The housekeeper grabbed her arm. "You need to stay until Mr. Win gets home. He'll iron the whole thing out. I'll bet my bottom dollar this is something Mrs. Whittaker cooked up. She always wanted Mr. Win to marry that snob."

"I'm sorry." Kenni heard a car horn. "My cab's here. I have to go. Anytime you get a hankering for grits, my house is open."

Donna grabbed the phone the minute Kenni walked out the door.

Chapter Thirty-Five

The bad news was that the meeting had lasted far longer than Win anticipated. The good news was it was going well. By the time it ended, the arrangements that would dramatically alter his professional and personal life would be complete.

The woman who'd wormed her way into his heart was about to turn his world on its head—new wife, new home, and a considerable deviation in the course of his professional life.

Kenni, her wacky friends, and her slightly eccentric family would be his when she said yes to his proposal. That question—and answer—would come as soon as he could get home. He patted his pocket and felt the small ring box. Soon, very soon, he'd have a diamond on her finger.

Win's interlude in D.C. had seemed like forever, but now Kenni was here. And much to his delight, Donna had bestowed her seal of approval.

If the yakking went on much longer he'd have to call it quits. He had plans to make and a pretty lady to kiss.

The party would serve several functions, both personal and professional. On the business side, he wanted to use the opportunity to explain the reconfiguration of the firm.

On the fun side, he couldn't wait to introduce Kenni to his friends and colleagues. He had no doubt they'd be charmed and envious. His plans were in place, and now all he had to do was get home to pop the question.

Colby was about to start on the second chorus of yada, yada, yada when Win's secretary slipped into the conference room.

"Mr. Whittaker," she whispered, "your housekeeper called and said you have to get home right now. Your guest left."

At first he couldn't make any sense of what she was saying. "Who has left?"

"She said Miss McAllister took a cab to the airport."

That got his attention. "Colby, I've got to go, something's happening at home." He didn't wait for an answer before he sprinted out the door.

"DONNA, DONNA," Win bellowed, running into the house. "What happened? Why did Kenni leave?"

"I think it was that Amelie woman." Donna underlined her allegation with a snort. "She's here all dressed up and bossing the caterers around. Miss Kenni said Amelie told her you two were getting engaged."

"What?"

"She's still in the dining room if you want to talk to her."

"You bet I do." Amelie Barrois was a pain in the rear. To say she threw herself at him was putting it mildly. It all started when he'd made the mistake of going to her family home in France. From that point on, she assumed they would eventually get married. Then he made the even bigger blunder of dating her. That was when his mother had started shopping for wedding invitations.

Win stomped down the hall. He was aching for a fight but trying like heck to control his temper. Getting mad at Amelie tended to send her into hysterics—and that was the last thing he needed. His mother, however, was going to get a piece of his mind. This mess had her fingerprints all over it.

"What have you done this time?" That was reasonably calm.

"Why hello, darling. I knew you needed some help with your party, so I came over early." Amelie had simpering down to a fine art.

"Why don't you sit down? We need to talk." Hanging on to his composure by a thread, Win continued. "I want you to know that I'm planning to marry Kenni McAllister." He emphasized the point by pulling the ring case out of his pocket. "So I want you to tell me precisely what you said to her."

Amelie smiled. "I just pointed out that I usually serve as your hostess and I may have hinted we're going to announce our engagement tonight. Your mother told me about the party and everything else."

Yep, his mom was the villain in this piece. "I don't care what my mother thinks. I'm only going to say this once. We are not getting engaged, not now, not ever. You're being delusional if you think otherwise. I want you to leave." His limited patience was almost at an end. "If you're not gone in about three seconds, I'm going to toss your butt out on the street."

Nope, calm and quiet wasn't his forte. That's exactly the reason he hadn't gone into the diplomatic corps. Win ignored Amelie's declarations of love as he stalked to the phone. Where was the stupid phone book?

He spied Donna lurking at the dining room door. "Please pack me a bag and then call Colby and tell him what's happened. He'll have to play host for me tonight."

Win was in for some world-class groveling. So bring it on! He was ready.

KENNI FELT like a bag lady. Her eyes were red and swollen, her head was about to burst and she generally felt like crap, with a capital *C*.

Although it wasn't late when they landed in Atlanta, it had been a long and *very* eventful day, and other than renting a car Kenni didn't have any way to get home.

The shuttle didn't run at night, and she wasn't up to dealing with her friends or family members. They were so buttinski, they'd either be dripping in sympathy or they'd be ready to organize a necktie party.

Kenni briefly, very briefly, considered hopping the next plane to Timbuktu. That way when she finally got home, she could pretend she and Win had had a great time but mutually decided to call it quits. Nope. That was the chicken way to handle adversity, and Kenni McAllister was made of sterner stuff. She'd never clucked her way through a bad situation.

And if you believed that, the Brooklyn Bridge was for sale.

Rejecting a quick getaway to Cancun, she opted for a hotel room and worrying about explaining her early return tomorrow. She *so* did not want to look like an idiot!

Aargh! That was Kenni's version of a primal scream; actually, considering security and everything, it was more of a grunt, but you get the drift. This was not one of her better days.

Snag her luggage. Find a hotel. Get a grip! As far as self-motivation mantras went, that wasn't exactly the best, but it would have to do.

She followed the crowd to the chaotic baggage claim area. What was the carousel number? Jeez, if she couldn't remember something that simple, her belongings would likely be lost forever in the bowels of Hartsfield International Airport.

"Pardon me, pardon me, that one's mine. Would you grab it?" she exclaimed, as her suitcase slid by. Perhaps her luck had changed. Someone down the line hefted it off the belt. Hurray for Good Samaritans. However, when Good Sam dropped Kenni's bag at her feet, she almost had a coronary.

"What's a nice girl like you doing in a place like this?" Win didn't wait for her to answer before he continued. "Don't you think we have some things to talk about?"

This was *not* a rational girl's fantasy. She looked like a

derelict, and he was scrumptious enough to eat with a spoon. Where was the justice in that! And how did he get to Atlanta?

"Why aren't you at home?" That was a stupid thing to say. "I mean, what are you doing here?" Great, that was even more obtuse. Escape seemed to be the best option, so Kenni reached for the suitcase. Perhaps she could get outside and grab a cab before he realized what she was up to.

Win was smarter than that. "To answer your question, I flew in on a chartered plane. And nothing doing, you aren't going anywhere without me." He made a preemptive grab for the handle.

"Give me my bag," Kenni yelped. Uh-oh, people were staring. She grabbed the suitcase with both hands just as he released the handle and reached in his pocket. Yep, you got it—she landed on the floor with a splat.

"Miss, is there a problem?" The airport security guy was not amused. Great! Wouldn't that be the icing on the cake? They could get arrested for brawling in baggage claim.

"I'm sorry, Officer, we were just clowning around. Truly, there's nothing to be concerned about." She gave the man with the gun one of her biggest smiles, and quickly discovered that most of her fellow travelers had abandoned any pretense of disinterest and were blatantly staring.

The way the cop was glaring at Win she was afraid he was about to read him his Miranda rights. "Are you positive there isn't a problem?" He turned his attention back to Kenni.

"Absolutely, but thank you anyway."

"Okay, if you're sure." Spearing Win with a final look, the security guard strolled to the escalator.

"Let's get out of here. We can finish this fight someplace private," she hissed.

"That sounds like a plan to me," he replied, grabbing the handle of her bag.

Kenni didn't have much of a choice but to follow, and surprisingly he didn't head to a limo, or a shuttle, or even a taxi. He went straight downstairs to the MARTA, Atlanta's version of mass transit.

"Where are we going?" Kenni asked as she got on the train.

"We're going to a hotel."

"No, we're not. Not with me looking like this." She opened her arms in an all-encompassing gesture.

Win gave her one of his knee-knocking smiles and pushed an errant lock of hair behind her ear. "I had a wonderful plan that included roses and champagne, but it seems I misplaced the most important player. So to say it like a true Southerner, the romance thing ain't gonna happen."

He got down on one knee, ignoring the filth on the floor. The next thing she knew, he was holding a small black velvet box.

"What's that?" Her voice went up an octave. Damn it, she hated when she sounded like Minnie Mouse. What a dim-witted question. Of course she recognized a ring box.

Win flipped open the lid to reveal a diamond the size of a large marble.

"Kenni McAllister, I want you to be my wife, for now and for always. I love you. Do you love me?"

"Oh, yeah." In the annals of affirmative answers, that wasn't exactly Shakespearian, but hey, it worked.

"If you hadn't run off, you would've found out that I've made plans to move to Magnolia Bluffs."

"Why?" she whispered. How could a slick big-city lawyer find happiness in a small Southern town?

"Because I love you and we're meant to be together." He slid his finger down her cheek.

Good answer. Actually, it wasn't merely good, it was the very best.

"I am so sorry I messed this up. I should've told you what I was planning."

She had to agree with that.

"So," he said with a grin, "will you marry me—even if I do have a terrible sense of timing? We can live in your house, or buy a house, or whatever you want."

She stopped his rambling with a resounding *yes.* Her answer was enthusiastic enough to wake the drunk at the end of the train car. That was the last thing she noticed before he sealed their agreement with a long, lazy kiss.

Epilogue

"This is what I call a bridesmaid's dress." Liza did a twirl showing off her cobalt-blue sheath. "I can wear it to a fancy restaurant," she announced. "Not that I ever have a date, but hope springs eternal."

"You look gorgeous, and so do I," her twin said. "And the bride is stunning."

Win and Kenni had decided on a no-frills wedding, so the nuptials were to be held at the gazebo. They felt it was the most appropriate setting, since General Joe Johnston had witnessed their first kiss.

"Do I look okay?" Kenni asked. "Honest answer." Of course she did. They'd foraged through every retail establishment in Atlanta until they'd finally found the perfect outfit...at Steinmart's. It wasn't exactly haute couture, but it was beautiful. And even better, it was cheap.

"You couldn't be any prettier," Maizie said through her tears. "Group hug."

When the ladies finally disengaged themselves, Liza wiped her eyes. "And don't worry, we won't tell your new mother-in-law, the one who bought her dress in Paris, where we found this number." She fingered the soft pale peach silk of Kenni's sheath.

"Okay, I guess I'm ready. Make sure I don't have any mascara under my eyes. I don't want raccoon eyes in our pictures."

"Check, no raccoon eyes. Now let's bustle to the gazebo and get you married."

Uncle Dave chauffeured them in his squad car, lights blazing. Kenni felt it was appropriate, since they'd been instrumental in solving the only unexplained death to happen in the county in the past ten years. Heck, they should've gotten a badge for their efforts. Mama would've been so proud, and she'd *love* Win.

Oops, tears threatened to reappear. Tears of happiness. Kenni thought about her husband-to-be. He was sexy, fun and the love of her life. The sun was shining, flowers were in bloom, she had fantastic family and friends, and best of all, she was marrying the greatest guy in the world.

All in all, things couldn't get much better.

"Here we are, girls." Dave announced the bridal party's arrival with a blare of the siren.

Aunt Eugenie knocked on his window and when he rolled it down she let him have it. "I've told you over and over not to do that. I thought I was going to have to do CPR on Mrs. Stackhouse. And if I was forced to blow in that woman's mouth, you would have never heard the end of it."

He looked sheepish, but he was still grinning.

"We have a wedding to attend," Liza said, jumping out of the car, pulling Kenni with her.

When Kenni started down the aisle, accompanied by Anna Belle and Joe and Dave and Eugenie, Raylene and Toolie whooped and hollered to beat the band. Even her soon-to-be in-laws got into the spirit of things. Who would ever have suspected you could mingle collard greens and pâté de foie gras? And Colby, the man who'd started it all, had Kristen Whittaker on his arm and a silly grin on his face.

Tears of joy misted Kenni's eyes. There he was—tall, handsome and hers forever.

And those tears spilled over during the vows, when he held Kenni's hand and proudly announced, "I'm permanently yours."

* * * * *

ANN DEFEE has made a name for herself with the Southern charm and wacky humor of her American Romance novels.

In SUMMER AFTER SUMMER, her first story for Harlequin Everlasting Love, she expands her repertoire—without losing her trademark style.

This story is about the lifelong love between Jasmine Boudreaux and Charlie Morrison. It starts when they're teenagers in 1973 and ends today (although their love will go on!).

Turn the page for an excerpt from
SUMMER AFTER SUMMER
and you'll see what we mean!
SUMMER AFTER SUMMER
is available wherever Harlequin books are sold.

Chapter 1

"Jasmine Boudreaux! You girls watch out for snakes now, ya hear?" Mama's honeyed drawl drifted over the languid green river to the wooden raft where I was sunbathing with my three best friends—Bunny Bennett, Mary Alice Cunningham and Misty Stewart.

Although we were as different as the four points of the compass, we'd been best buddies since our first day in kinder-garten. Mary Alice was thoughtful, sensitive and more than a little religious. Bunny, the wild child, was on the opposite end of the spectrum. And Misty was our version of intelligentsia, bouncing back and forth between arcane ideologies. One day you'd find her quoting Ayn Rand; the next she'd be reading Karl Marx.

And speaking of dichotomies—I was a walking, talking Gemini. Although I was the most pragmatic member of our group, I was naive enough to fall for every practical joke in the universe.

I was fairly sure Mary Alice and I were the only two virgins in our senior class. I say that tentatively because virginity, or lack of it, was one of the few things we didn't discuss.

"Bucky said he saw at least half a dozen moccasins in the river last night, and you know how those nasty things like to get up on that old dock to sun."

"Yes, Mama, we'll be careful," I replied, although I didn't bother to open my eyes. Through some strange quirk of fate, Bucky was my brother. He was a junior at the University of Texas and he was absolutely positive he was the grand pooh-bah of the Western world. Truth be told, he was a pain in the rear.

Bunny sat up and engaged Mama in conversation—an exceptionally bad idea, since my mother loved to talk.

"Miz Boudreaux, did my mom call?" Bunny could put on the thickest Texas accent you ever heard. And this was one of those occasions.

"No, honey, she hasn't. What do you want me to tell her if she does?" Mama had to yell in order to be heard.

"Just remind her I'm spending the night here, if you would. Not that she really cares where I am." That last sentence was meant strictly for our ears.

"Sure thing, honey," Mama agreed. "Jazzy, we're eating at the country club, so you girls go to the Pink Pig for supper. I'll leave some money on the kitchen table."

In Meadow Lake, Texas, population 8,631, the Pink Pig Burger Emporium was the "happening" place. Happening, that is, if you were into junk food, teenagers and the occasional redneck—"happening" of course, being a relative term.

Growing up in a small south Texas town when your daddy's the police chief presented some challenges. Everyone, and I do mean everyone, thought it was their job to report my every move. Swear to goodness, if I'd been audacious enough to utter the f-word, Mama would've known about it before I closed my mouth.

Every weekend, the kids had this ritual where we all circled the Pink Pig, cruised to the park on the other side of town, came back around to check out the movie theater, swung by Garcia's Pizzeria and then completed the circuit with a trip back to the PP. Around and around we went in a relentless circle of teenager hormones.

I was so busy thinking about life in the high-school zone that I almost missed the fact that Mama was still dispensing advice from the shore.

"Misty, you watch out and don't get sunburned. With your red hair, you could blister right up." Mama was well into her drill-sergeant routine.

"Yes, ma'am," the redhead in question yelled as she rolled over and smeared more baby oil on her exposed stomach. "Maybe if I get my freckles to run together I'll be able to tan. What do ya think?" she asked, even though we all knew it was a rhetorical question.

Misty had been trying to tan since the fourth grade and she'd never progressed beyond the burn, peel and freckle stage. I, on the other hand, had the skin of my Cajun ancestors and by the end of the summer I was as brown as a berry. It was one of those things that made her crazy.

One of the benefits of living in a small town was that you could have lifelong friends. We'd shared everything—our thoughts, our dreams and on occasion our communicable diseases. The only exception to the "share and share alike" rule was boyfriends. But that's a story I'll get to later.

Bunny's dad owned a tractor factory, which employed half the people in town. She was our bouncy blonde. The bouncy part came naturally; the blondness was courtesy of a bottle.

The Bennetts were filthy rich and loved to flaunt it. Mrs.

Bennett's diamonds rivaled the crown jewels. And that marble mausoleum Bunny called home was totally sterile.

Misty's parents were professors. They had to be book-smart or they wouldn't be teaching at the college. However, I thought their general IQ was questionable. Sometimes they treated their only child as if she'd just popped in from another planet.

Mary Alice was a total sweetheart. A bit clueless in the fashion department, but one of the nicest people you could meet. Her dad was a Holy Roller preacher—need I say more?

So now you have an idea why we spent so much time at my house. My parents were cool, most of the time anyway, plus we had a ski boat. And for some unfathomable reason Misty had a major-league crush on Bucky. Just thinking about Misty and Bucky doing anything vaguely erotic exceeded my yuck factor.

We were freshly minted high-school graduates and feeling invincible. Actually, that wasn't quite the truth, at least for me. I was terrified. In a moment of insanity I'd applied to the school of architecture at UC Berkeley—that's in California—and to my amazement I was accepted. It seemed like a good idea when I was filling out the application, but California, good grief!

What *was* I thinking?

"Jazzy! You're daydreaming again." Misty put her thumb over the lip of her Coke bottle and pretended to spray me. "I have a rumor to spread."

"Wow," the rest of the group said in chorus. Misty was usually the last person to know anything. Not that she was ditzy; she just didn't pay much attention to gossip.

"I overheard my mother on the phone talking to Dean Patrick. She was whispering, but I got the drift of the conversation. Sandy Sorenson is getting married. Her daddy's on the faculty, you know." She paused for dramatic effect. "Sandy *has* to get married!"

"Sandy Sorenson," Mary Alice whispered. "Oh, my God, she is *so* beautiful."

Sandy was in her freshman year at the University of Texas, and rumor had it she'd taken the campus by storm.

"Who's the guy?" Not that I was prone to telling tales, but I figured we might as well get all the facts.

"I don't know. When Mom saw me she went into the laundry room and closed the door." Misty frowned. "Isn't it awful that Sandy has to get married?"

Her comment sent me into my women's-lib mode. "Why would anyone 'have' to get married in this day and age? Please!" Talk about making me crazy. We weren't living in the 1950s. *I Love Lucy* and its archaic view of sex was nothing more than a TV rerun.

I was about to continue my rant when I noticed that Bunny was curiously silent. Usually she was the first to jump in on a good story.

Mary Alice piped up instead. "A baby needs parents who are married."

Our sweet little friend was getting annoyed. Normally she was fairly open-minded, but on the topic of babies and pregnancy her church background came to the fore.

"Billy Tom said he's ready for tonight," Bunny commented. That girl was the queen of the non sequitur, and this was a subject that definitely needed to be changed.

So Sandy Sorenson took a backseat while we discussed our upcoming adventure. Although it took some world-class whee-dling, we'd finally convinced our buddy Billy Tom to help us get drunk for the first time. As a group, we had a well-earned reputa-tion for being Goody Two-shoes—no booze and no pot. Since we were all heading to college, we'd decided to take a walk on the wild side…in a safe environment. And you couldn't get much safer than being with Billy Tom. It wasn't so much that he was benign; it was the fact that we had a ton of blackmail material on him.

"He paid some guy five bucks to buy us three six-packs. That's four apiece." Bunny was our soiree coordinator. "I'm not sure any of us will be coherent after four beers."

Neither was I, but what did I know? Most of the kids went out to the river to drink and neck and God only knew what else. Daddy was well aware of the kegger parties and periodically sent a deputy to patrol the area. Needless to say, I had *never* attended one. If my daddy had caught me there, I would've been grounded until I qualified for Social Security, and that wasn't in my game plan. I had people to see and places to go.

"What did you tell Charlie we were doing tonight?" Mary Alice directed her question to Bunny. She was referring to Bunny's boyfriend, who was, unfortunately, the love of my life. But that was a secret I wasn't about to share with anyone, not even my best friends, or to be more specific, *especially* not my best friends. Charlie, darn it, treated me like his buddy.

Charlie Morrison and Bunny had been a couple for almost a year, and in my opinion it was an ill-fated liaison. The Bennetts despised him, more than likely because he wasn't rich and his family wasn't socially prominent.

When Bunny and Charlie first started going out, her parents made the mistake of issuing an ultimatum, which was like waving a red flag at a bull. Tell the girl she couldn't do something, and she went full steam ahead. So all year she used her friends as an excuse to get out of the house.

I'd known Charlie's parents almost my entire life and I thought they were fantastic. They owned a fishing camp/restaurant down the road from our house. Looking back, I suppose it was little more than a beer joint, but Mrs. Morrison's Friday night hush puppies and fried catfish bash was famous throughout the county.

I'll never forget when I met the Morrison twins. It was my first day of school and Mama made a huge production about me riding the school bus. That was also the day Bubba Hawkins decided to make my life a living hell.

To give it a nice spin, he was a big, fat bully, and like all tyrants he homed in on the vulnerable. What he hadn't expected was

Charlie Morrison. After Charlie and Colton, his fraternal twin, got through with Bubba he never bothered me again. That was the day I fell in love with Charlie.

When we were in elementary school, the Morrison twins and I spent most of our summer days playing cops and robbers in the pecan orchard by the lake. Colton was a great buddy, but even then I knew Charlie was special.

It seemed as if my entire life consisted of a collage of Charlie memories. He risked life and limb teaching me to water-ski—I wasn't the most coordinated person in the world. And when I got my learner's permit he instructed me in the art of driving a stick shift. Again, a scary proposition.

But it was in the pecan orchard on a sultry summer night after our freshman year that he truly stole my heart. That was my first kiss, and what a kiss it was. My life would never be the same. Too bad he didn't feel the same way. Darn it, the idiot never kissed me again!

"I told him I was busy. He got all snotty. He'll just have to deal with it. It's not like we're joined at the hip," Bunny groused.

If Charlie wanted to stick to *me* like glue, I'd have been a happy, happy girl. But he was a passion I needed to ditch, because obviously it didn't have a chance in h-e-double toothpicks of going anywhere. We were another Romeo and Juliet, except in this case Romeo wasn't enamored of Juliet.

So there I was, a seventeen-year-old virgin (in more ways than one) beer-drinker planning to sneak off to the drive-in with a bunch of girls to slurp suds. And we were going to pull off this great misadventure in Billy Tom's '57 Plymouth that didn't even have a working radio.

How pitiful was that?

* * * * *

Welcome to cowboy country...

Turn the page for a sneak preview of
TEXAS BABY
by
Kathleen O'Brien
An exciting new title from Harlequin Superromance
for everyone who loves stories about the West.

Harlequin Superromance—
Where life and love weave together in
emotional and unforgettable ways.

CHAPTER ONE

CHASE TRANSFERRED his gaze to the road and identified a foreign spot on the horizon. A car. Almost half a mile away, where the straight, tree-lined drive met the public road. He could tell it was coming too fast, but judging the speed of a vehicle moving straight toward you was tricky.

It wasn't until it was about two hundred yards away that he realized the driver must be drunk...or crazy. Or both.

The guy was going maybe sixty. On a private drive, out here in ranch country, where kids or horses or tractors or stupid chickens might come darting out any minute, that was criminal. Chase straightened from his comfortable slouch and waved his hands.

"Slow down, you fool," he called out. He took the porch steps quickly and began walking fast down the driveway.

The car veered oddly, from one lane to another, then up onto the slight rise of the thick green spring grass. It just barely missed the fence.

"Slow down, damn it!"

He couldn't see the driver, and he didn't recognize this automobile. It was small and old, and couldn't have cost much even when it was new. It was probably white, but now it needed either a wash or a new paint job or both.

"Damn it, what's wrong with you?"

At the last minute, he had to jump away, because the idiot behind the wheel clearly wasn't going to turn to avoid a collision. He couldn't believe it. The car kept coming, finally slowing a little, but it was too late.

Still going about thirty miles an hour, it slammed into the large, white-brick pillar that marked the front boundaries of the house. The pillar wasn't going to give an inch, so the car had to. The front end folded up like a paper fan.

It seemed to take forever for the car to settle, as if the trauma happened in slow motion, reverberating from the front to the back of the car in ripples of destruction. The front windshield suddenly seemed to ice over with lethal bits of glassy frost. Then the side windows exploded.

The front driver's door wrenched open, as if the car wanted to expel its contents. Metal buckled hideously. Small pieces, like hubcaps and mirrors, skipped and ricocheted insanely across the oyster-shell driveway.

Finally, everything was still. Into the silence, a plume of steam shot up like a geyser, smelling of rust and heat. Its snake-like hiss almost smothered the low, agonized moan of the driver.

Chase's anger had disappeared. He didn't feel anything but a dull sense of disbelief. Things like this didn't happen in real life. Not in his life. Maybe the sun had actually put him to sleep....

But he was already kneeling beside the car. The driver was a woman. The frosty glass-ice of the windshield was dotted with small flecks of blood. She must have hit it with her head, because just below her hairline a red liquid was seeping out. He touched it. He tried to wipe it away before it reached her eyebrow, though, of course that made no sense at all. Her eyes were shut.

Was she conscious? Did he dare move her? Her dress was covered in glass, and the metal of the car was sticking out lethally in all the wrong places.

Then he remembered, with an intense relief, that every good medical man in the county was here, just behind the house, drinking his champagne. He found his phone and paged Trent.

The woman moaned again.

Alive, then. Thank God for that.

He saw Trent coming toward him, starting out at a lope, but quickly switching to a full run.

"Get Dr. Marchant," Chase called. "Don't bother with 911."

Trent didn't take long to assess the situation. A fraction of a second, and he began pulling out his cell phone and running toward the house.

The yelling seemed to have roused the woman. She opened her eyes. They were blue and clouded with pain and confusion.

"Chase," she said.

His breath stalled. His head pulled back. "What?"

Her only answer was another moan, and he wondered if he had imagined the word. He reached around her and put his arm behind her shoulders. She was tiny. Probably petite by nature, but surely way too thin. He could feel her shoulder blades pushing against her skin, as fragile as the wishbone in a turkey.

She seemed to have passed out, so he put his other arm under her knees and lifted her out. He tried to avoid the jagged metal, but her skirt caught on a piece and the tearing sound seemed to wake her again.

"No," she said. "Please."

"I'm just trying to help," he said. "It's going to be all right."

She seemed profoundly distressed. She wriggled in his arms, and she was so weak, like a broken bird. It made him feel too big and brutish. And intrusive. As if touching her this way, his bare hands against the warm skin behind her knees, were somehow a transgression.

He wished he could be more delicate. But he smelled gasoline, and he knew it wasn't safe to leave her here.

Finally he heard the sound of voices, as guests began to run around the side of the house, alerted by Trent. Dr. Marchant was at the front, racing toward them as if he were forty instead of seventy. Susannah was right behind him, her green dress floating around her trim legs.

"Please," the woman in his arms murmured again. She looked at him, the expression in her blue eyes lost and bewildered. He wondered if she might be on drugs. Hitting her head on the windshield might account for this unfocused, glazed look, but it couldn't explain the crazy driving.

"Please, put me down. Susannah… The wedding…"

Chase's arms tightened instinctively, and he froze in his tracks. She whimpered, and he realized he might be hurting her. "Say that again?"

"The wedding. I have to stop it."

* * * * *

Be sure to look for TEXAS BABY,
available September 11, 2007,
as well as other fantastic Superromance titles
available in September.

HARLEQUIN®
Super Romance®

Welcome to Cowboy Country...

TEXAS BABY
by Kathleen O'Brien

#1441

Chase Clayton doesn't know what to think.
A beautiful stranger has just crashed his
engagement party, demanding that he not
marry because she's pregnant with his baby.
But the kicker is—he's never seen her before.

Look for TEXAS BABY and other fantastic
Superromance titles on sale September 2007.

Available wherever books are sold.

HARLEQUIN®
Super Romance®

**Where life and love weave together
in emotional and unforgettable ways.**

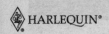

Every great love has a story to tell™

Third time's a charm.

Texas summers. Charlie Morrison.
Jasmine Boudreaux has always connected
the two. Her relationship with Charlie
begins and ends in high school. Twenty
years later it begins again—and ends again.
Now fate has stepped in one more time—
will Jazzy and Charlie finally give in to
the love they've shared all this time?

Look for

Summer After Summer
by
Ann DeFee

**Available September
wherever books are sold.**

HESAS0907

REQUEST YOUR FREE BOOKS!
2 FREE NOVELS PLUS 2
FREE GIFTS!

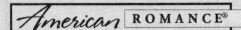

Heart, Home & Happiness!

YES! Please send me 2 FREE Harlequin American Romance® novels and my 2 FREE gifts. After receiving them, if I don't wish to receive any more books, I can return the shipping statement marked "cancel." If I don't cancel, I will receive 4 brand-new novels every month and be billed just $4.24 per book in the U.S., or $4.99 per book in Canada, plus 25¢ shipping and handling per book and applicable taxes, if any*. That's a savings of close to 15% off the cover price! I understand that accepting the 2 free books and gifts places me under no obligation to buy anything. I can always return a shipment and cancel at any time. Even if I never buy another book from Harlequin, the two free books and gifts are mine to keep forever.

154 HDN EEZK   354 HDN EEZV

Name _____ (PLEASE PRINT) _____

Address _____ Apt. # _____

City _____ State/Prov. _____ Zip/Postal Code _____

Signature (if under 18, a parent or guardian must sign) _____

Mail to the **Harlequin Reader Service®**:
IN U.S.A.: P.O. Box 1867, Buffalo, NY 14240-1867
IN CANADA: P.O. Box 609, Fort Erie, Ontario L2A 5X3

Not valid to current Harlequin American Romance subscribers.

Want to try two free books from another line?
Call 1-800-873-8635 or visit www.morefreebooks.com.

* Terms and prices subject to change without notice. NY residents add applicable sales tax. Canadian residents will be charged applicable provincial taxes and GST. This offer is limited to one order per household. All orders subject to approval. Credit or debit balances in a customer's account(s) may be offset by any other outstanding balance owed by or to the customer. Please allow 4 to 6 weeks for delivery.

Your Privacy: Harlequin is committed to protecting your privacy. Our Privacy Policy is available online at www.eHarlequin.com or upon request from the Reader Service. From time to time we make our lists of customers available to reputable firms who may have a product or service of interest to you. If you would prefer we not share your name and address, please check here. ☐

HAR07

ATHENA FORCE

Heart-pounding romance
and thrilling adventure.

Professional negotiator Lindsey Novak
is faced with her biggest challenge—to
buy back Teal Arnett, a young woman with
unique powers. In the process Lindsey
uncovers a devastating plot that involves
scientists from around the globe, and all of
them lead to one woman who is bent on
destroying Athena Academy…at any cost.

LOOK FOR

THE GOOD THIEF
by Judith Leon

*Available September
wherever you buy books.*

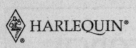

HARLEQUIN®

American ROMANCE®

COMING NEXT MONTH

#1177 TWIN SURPRISE by Jacqueline Diamond
Times Two

Marta Lawson is secretly in love with police officer and playboy Derek Reed.
When her friends put in a bid at a bachelor auction, her birthday present turns
out to be a few glorious hours with the town lady-killer! It's a fantasy come
true—except about a month later she finds her "dream" date has resulted in not
one surprise, but two....

#1178 DANCING WITH DALTON by Laura Marie Altom
Fatherhood

Dance instructor Rose Vasquez was widowed two years ago, and even though her
six-year-old daughter lights up her life, her world is not complete. Buying a dance
studio allows Rose to throw herself into teaching, but she never expected to find
amongst her new students a man who makes her feel so gloriously alive....

#1179 HOME FOR A HERO by Mary Anne Wilson
Shelter Island Stories

Lucas Roman had retreated to Shelter Island to heal wounds he'd suffered in
his tour of duty. Physically, he was fine, but the reason he'd chosen exile was a
closely guarded secret. Lucas thought he had his new life worked out, but then
his prized solitude was shattered by Shay Donovan, a woman who, literally,
invaded his private beach....

#1180 ONE STUBBORN TEXAN by Kara Lennox

Russ Klein has a perfect small-town life—until a big-city detective named
Sydney Baines discovers he's a long-lost heir with a big inheritance. Preserving
his family means refusing the money, which also means asking the dainty sleuth
to forget he exists. But Sydney has her own reasons for needing Russ to take the
money—and she's not backing down!

www.eHarlequin.com

HARCNM0807